Ju
F
K18   Kay, Mara.
          In face of danger.

Ju
F
K18   Kay, Mara.
          In face of danger.

In Face of Danger

In Face of Danger

By Mara Kay

Crown Publishers, Inc., New York

Published in the United States in 1977.
Copyright © 1976 by Mara Kay.
Published in Great Britain in 1976 under the title *Storm Warning*.
All rights reserved. No part of this publication may be reproduced, stored in a retrieval system, or transmitted, in any form or by any means, electronic, mechanical, photocopying, recording, or otherwise, without prior written permission of the publisher. Inquiries should be addressed to Crown Publishers, Inc., One Park Avenue, New York, N.Y. 10016
Manufactured in the United States of America

10 9 8 7 6 5 4 3 2 1

The text of this book is set in 12 pt. Baskerville.

LIBRARY OF CONGRESS CATALOGING IN PUBLICATION DATA

Kay, Mara.   In face of danger.
SUMMARY: While residing with a German family, English-born Ann Lindsay discovers that Frau Meixner, whose son is a member of the Hitler Youth, is hiding two Jewish girls in the attic.   [1. Jews in Germany—Fiction]   I. Title.
PZ7.K198I1   [Fic]   77-21949
ISBN 0-517-53119-4

Contents

In Face of Danger

1

The Green Room

The room was slowly coming out of the fog. First the blur on the ceiling took shape and became a lamp of green glass that looked like an overturned umbrella. Then the walls emerged, covered with faded green-striped wallpaper. Here and there were little hanging shelves holding a china elephant, two kissing doves, and a vase with two paper roses.

Lying with her head deep in pillows, Ann watched the fog sink lower and lower until she could see a tall wooden footboard with a blue towel thrown over it. She squinted a little and saw two arms, one bandaged, stretched across the green blanket. It took her some time to realize that the arms were her own.

I must have been in an accident, Ann thought. "But

how?" she said aloud. She did not recognize her own voice in the croaky whisper that came out. "I was . . . I was . . ." She broke off, watching the fingers of her un-bandaged hand pluck at the blanket. I don't even know where I am.

Seized by a sudden suffocating feeling of panic, she kicked her feet and after a desperate struggle pulled her-self into a sitting position. This was a mistake. A sharp pain shot through her right shoulder and a sudden wave of nausea mounted from the pit of her stomach into her mouth, filling it with a bitter taste.

She sank back. Around her the walls tilted and the green lamp swung dizzily. She closed her eyes and waited for the bed to stop rocking.

When she dared to open her eyes again, everything was standing still. She could see a window with a lacy white curtain tied back with a green silk cord. Underneath the window stood a big oak chair with two embroidered cushions. From the swish of tires and the sound of foot-steps on the pavement outside, Ann guessed that the room must overlook the street, but all she could see was a patch of gray sky and a wet branch swaying in the wind.

I must not panic, she told herself. At least I know who I am. My name is Ann Lindsay. I am English. I was . . . She felt cold sweat break out at the nape of her neck. Her mind groped, searched, struggled, but everything was blank. She took a deep breath. It helped, but deep breathing hurt her chest. She lay very quietly, waiting for the pain to ebb away, and heard the distant singing.

Die Fahne hoch! Die Reihen dicht geschlossen!
S.A. marschiert mit ruhig festem Schritt . . .

Ann listened. She knew what they were singing:

4

The flags high! Close the ranks!
S.A. are marching with calm firm step . . .

The words floated to her, sometimes muffled, sometimes clear . . .

Die Strasse frei den braunen Battalionen!
Die Strasse frei . . .

Again her mind registered the meaning:

Clear the street for the brown battalions!
Clear the street . . .

The song died away in the distance, then came again,
accompanied by the sound of cadenced steps, as if a whole
crowd was marching. Nearer, nearer:

Zum letztenmal wird nun Appell geblasen.
Zum Kampfe stehen wir le schon bereit.
Bald flattern Hitlerfahnen uber alle Strassen,
Die Knechtschaft dauert nur noch kurze Zeit.

For the last time the appeal is sounded!
We are all ready for the fight.
Soon will Hitler's flags fly over all the streets,
The slavery will last only for a short time more.

Why were the words different from their meaning?
Abruptly the singing stopped. Marching steps were re-
placed by the clicking of heels. A man's voice shouted,
"Heil Hitler!" and a chorus of boyish voices answered,
"Heil Hitler!" After a moment of tense silence, came the
command, *"Abgetreten!"* There was laughter, shouting,
and the pounding of running feet on the pavement.
A door banged somewhere very close, probably in the

5

house because the floor under Ann's bed shuddered and creaked. She paid no attention to it. Her memory was coming back. The recollections surged up, tumbling over each other. She knew it would take time to sort them out, make them fit into a coherent whole, but she searched desperately for something, anything that would help her to find out how she came to be in this unfamiliar green room.

The recollections were still chaotic, but Ann forced herself to concentrate. There was a car . . . Uncle Dick's car! He was driving and she was in the front seat with him. He said . . . he said . . . Her mind stumbled, then suddenly started to race. Now she could almost hear Uncle Dick's voice saying, "Yes, Frankfurt is fascinating. The whole of Germany is fascinating, but it's becoming uncomfortable. Just as well we're leaving." Did she answer? Probably not. There was no time. A large truck was bearing down on them, veering from side to side of the street as if totally out of control. Uncle Dick spun the wheel and tried to swerve, but it was too late. The truck was already towering over them. Ann felt herself flung violently forward. The last thing she saw was a street sign with *Mylius Strasse* in white against dark blue. Then blackness came.

That was it, then. She must have been hurt and carried into someone's house. Whatever had happened to her must have been serious because she was feeling so terribly weak.

She closed her eyes, only to open them wide again as a sudden thought cut through her brain like a knife. Uncle Dick? Was he hurt too? Or maybe . . . Oh, no!

Straining every muscle, she swung her feet out of bed. The room promptly started to spin again, but she ig-

6

nored it and put one foot onto the floor. Then the walls seemed to crumble. A slight sound came from the direction of the door, but she could not turn her head. Half in, half out of bed, all she could do was cling to the mattress to save herself from falling. She tried to call for help, but only a whisper came. She was about to let go when the door opened. Someone's arms picked her up bodily and laid her on the bed.

The minute she was on her back, Ann felt better. She blinked and saw a woman tucking in the sheets at the foot of the bed. Her back was turned to Ann, showing only a bunchy brown wool skirt that did not quite meet a magenta pullover. Topping the pullover was a mass of puffed-up red hair streaked with gray.

I must ask her about Uncle Dick, Ann thought. *"Bitte,"* she began. But her mind was too jumbled up to find the right German words, so she went on in English, even though she realized the woman might not understand her. "Please . . . tell me. The gentleman in the car? Where is he?" She could not bring herself to ask, "Is he alive?"

At the sound of Ann's urgent whisper, the woman turned toward her. Her heavily powdered, somewhat pudgy face looked anxious at first then relaxed into a smile. "Herr Lindsay? He in hospital is. Hurt here." She touched her back. "Herr Doctor Fromm say four, five *wochen* . . . weeks, all right again." She smoothed the blanket and rearranged the pillows. "To worry you must not," she added kindly.

"But . . . please . . . what happened? Why am I here? Where . . . where is this? You can speak German. I understand it."

The woman seemed only too glad to use her own lan-

7

guage. Speaking rapidly and gesturing a good deal, she told Ann that her name was Frau Meixner and that she had been sweeping her front steps last Tuesday morning when there was a bang and she saw a big truck collide with a small foreign car.

"Last Tuesday?" Ann interrupted. "What is today?"

"Friday, October the seventh," Frau Meixner answered simply.

"Then I've been unconscious for *three days!*"

Frau Meixner patted her hand and said soothingly in English, "Is all right. Herr Doctor Fromm say only concussion."

Ann managed to smile and Frau Meixner went back to her story and to German. Ann was glad of it. She found it much less tiring to follow than Frau Meixner's broken English. Not that there was much more to tell. People gathered around the wreck of the car, Frau Meixner said, and the police came. Ann had been thrown clear out through the windshield. A wonder she had not cut her face to pieces, but God is good. It would have been so terrible for a young girl. Uncle Dick was inside the car, but in the back seat. It was difficult to get him out because the car was on one side. It was the truck driver who finally wrenched the back door open. He was not hurt himself, but he was terribly upset and kept repeating he did not know why he had lost control of his vehicle.

Both Ann and Uncle Dick were unconscious but luckily Herr Doctor Fromm, Frau Meixner's next-door neighbor, had happened to be at home and heard the crash. Such a wonderful doctor and on the staff of a small private hospital. He immediately called the hospital and arranged for an ambulance to pick up Uncle Dick, but he thought it best not to move Ann so it was decided that

8

Frau Meixner would take her in. Also—*"Ah, Himmel!"* Frau Meixner interrupted herself as something metal crashed just outside the door and rolled clanging down the stairs.

Frau Meixner sighed. "It is my son Peter," she said. "Such a noisy boy! There is no afternoon school today because the Hitler's Youth is taking part in a parade. Parades instead of lessons!" Frau Meixner slapped her knee in disgust. "It is barely half an hour since he came home, and now he is off again to roller-skate with his friends and never mind if there are piles of leaves to be raked in the garden. Oh, well, eleven is a difficult age for a boy, especially when there is no father in the house. Peter was only four when my husband passed away."

Frau Meixner was talking on, but Ann was becoming more and more drowsy. She tried to say something, but her voice that seemed to become firmer while she was talking to Frau Meixner had now left her completely. The green room was fading away. She winced at the pain in her shoulder and fell asleep.

2
Looking Back

The next few days were a blur of sleeping and waking, mostly sleeping. Ann was aware of Frau Meixner coming in and out and occasionally she mustered up enough energy to eat a little, but the spoon soon dropped from her hand. Doctor Fromm came every evening, but by that time she was too sleepy to keep her eyes open. She was only dimly aware of his hands pressing her painful right shoulder and taking her pulse. It was difficult for the doctor to come in the daytime, Frau Meixner explained. He spent long hours in the hospital and often came home late at night. And why should he? What was there for him at home? He had no family except a stepsister who kept house for him. "A dear girl, but not quite right here." Frau Meixner tapped her forehead.

Ann listened with only half an ear. Doctor Fromm was taking care of Uncle Dick and that was all that mattered. She felt too ill to ask questions. But sometimes, during the day, she tried to imagine what Doctor Fromm looked like. He was very short, she decided, almost a dwarf, and very old, with a bald head and a long gray beard. She wondered how he could reach her when the bed was piled up so high on the feather mattress. Maybe he stood on a stool.

She was surprised and a tiny bit disappointed when one morning Frau Meixner ushered the doctor in and she saw a perfectly ordinary man of medium height, with a shock of dark hair that seemed to stand almost upright, and a clean-shaven face.

He's no older than Uncle Dick, she thought, then took another look and changed her mind. Uncle Dick did not have those weary lines at the corners of his eyes and around his mouth, or the tired expression of the man who stood leaning on the footboard of her bed.

"Good morning," Doctor Fromm said, speaking in English with only a slight accent. "Greetings from your uncle. He is much better, but it will take a few more weeks to make him quite well. How about yourself? I see that you have decided to wake up at last."

"Eh . . . yes," Ann stammered, thinking that even though the doctor's tone was cheerful, his voice sounded old and tired. "I don't feel so weak any more."

"Well, let me see." Doctor Fromm came over and gave Ann a brief examination. "You are getting better," he said approvingly, "I will give the good news to your uncle. He would have liked to talk to you, but I explained to him that Frau Meixner has no telephone upstairs."

11

"Couldn't I go downstairs?" Ann asked hopefully, but the doctor shook his finger at her. "Don't you dare!" he said. "We will proceed in easy steps. To begin with, you may sit in that armchair by the window for half an hour or so. Frau Meixner will help you to get up and put on a dressing gown. Oh, I almost forgot! Here is something to fatten you up. My sister made them." He put a plate tied up in a napkin on Ann's bedside table. "Did Frau Meixner say anything to you about Minna, I mean, my stepsister?" he asked, bending to untie the knots of the napkin.

As Ann hesitated, he said, sighing softly, "I see. Well, you will meet Minna sooner or later so I will tell you about her now, and then you will know all there is to know. Minna is twenty-four, but mentally she is only six. I was already a medical student when my father, a widower, married again. My stepmother was a widow and had a little girl. Minna was a bright child until she caught scarlet fever. There were complications and they affected her development. There!" He straightened up and showed Ann the plate heaped with little cakes covered with pink and white sugar icing.

"She made these herself!" Ann exclaimed. "But you said . . ."

"The good sisters of St. Gertrude's have done wonders for Minna," Doctor Fromm said. "They used to run a small school for retarded children in the old part of Frankfurt. Minna spent ten years there. They taught her to take care of herself, to cook, knit, and even to read. By this I mean she can read large type. She loves children's picture books."

"It must be a wonderful school," Ann murmured.

"*Was*," the doctor corrected. It was ordered to close

down last year. The Nazi regime does not approve of religious establishments, no matter how worthwhile. The nuns still maintain a small orphanage, but that won't last long either."

He stayed for a few more minutes, telling Ann about the two years he had spent in a medical school in London as an exchange student, and finally left, reminding her again not to rush things. At the door he turned and seemed about to say something more, but changed his mind and went out without speaking.

Walking from the bed to the chair by the window turned out to be quite a venture. Ann was glad enough to grasp Frau Meixner's arm as she walked with uneven steps across the green carpet. By the time the half hour was over she was longing to get back to bed.

It was easier the next day, and by the end of the week she spent most of her time sitting by the window, looking down at the quiet tree-lined street below. Frau Meixner brought her some English magazines and a deck of cards but it was pleasanter just to sit still, her hands in her lap, an old plaid blanket around her knees, and think.

The only difficulty was to organize her thoughts. She realized she should be thinking about the problems she and Uncle Dick were facing. Here they were in Germany for an indefinite time, existing—at least she was existing—on the kindness of a stranger, while Uncle Dick was in the hospital which must be running up all sorts of bills, and what would happen to his assignment? And how would she ever catch up at school?

The basic trouble was that this present time did not seem wholly real. None of it seemed wholly real, from the moment that Uncle Dick had appeared at the Rivington Academy for Girls and had quite calmly taken her away.

He was her legal guardian now, so he was entitled to remove her, but the school had made a terrible fuss. Thank goodness she was never going back there again. Uncle Dick had promised she could go back to her old school, though he did not believe in planning too far ahead. He said it was fatal in his profession since one never knew where the next story would surface and one had to be prepared to go anywhere in the world for an indefinite length of time. As he had been recalled from the Far East and was being sent to Germany to write a series of articles, he didn't see why he shouldn't take Ann with him to polish up her German and see a little of life. After all, he said, he was all the family she had left now, and vice versa. Ann had been cheered by that vice versa. Somehow it suggested that Uncle Dick really wanted to take her along to Germany with him.

She had felt a little shy during the first few days. Uncle Dick was her father's younger brother but he had seldom come to their house. She hardly knew him. When he had visited them, he tended to lecture her father about letting her do more things with other girls, join the Guides, or invite her friends to the house. He had urged them to consider boarding school for her. But her father had always answered, "I'm a sick man. I can't have a crowd of chattering schoolgirls around me, and I need Ann at home." Nor was it obvious that Uncle Dick's advice was right, for when she was sent to Rivington, after her father's death, she had hated it and longed only to be back in the quiet suburb with her own special friends at school.

Uncle Dick had been away when her father died, and it was almost two years before they met in the headmistress's study. He had looked older than she remembered

14

him: a middle-aged man, thinner than her father, but uncannily, heartwrenchingly, like him. This resemblance eased their first days together, for almost at once, it seemed, they were there, in Berlin.

She remembered staring through the plate glass window of the café to which Uncle Dick took her on the day they arrived. She was sipping hot chocolate with whipped cream and thinking with some disappointment that the throng of people passing on the pavement outside did not really look very different from people in England. Then there had come a pause in the traffic, and a line of big vehicles covered with burlap, with steel-helmeted men at the wheel, began to cross the intersection. On and on and on; it seemed to have no end.

Uncle Dick, who was scribbling in his notebook and drinking beer, looked up and put down his glass. "What do you think that was?" he asked when the last vehicle had vanished from sight.

"I don't know," Ann had answered, surprised by her uncle's serious tone. "Something military?"

"War material: tanks, gun carriages," Uncle Dick said in a low voice.

"War material?" Ann echoed. "But there is no war now."

"No, but it is coming, and soon."

Impressed and a little frightened by what she had just seen, Ann whispered, "Really? How do you know?"

"Look at the crowd around us and in the street. You are now Niece, Ward, and Sole Living Relative to a journalist, you must learn to notice things. What do you see?"

Ann stared out through the café window. She was not at all sure what Uncle Dick wanted her to notice. "Lots of men are wearing military uniform," she ventured.

Uncle Dick nodded approvingly. "Right. About three to one. Anything else?"

Ann had slouched in her seat, winding her legs tightly around the legs of her chair, and stared harder than ever. Usually this position helped her to concentrate, but it did not work this time. "I don't see anything else," she admitted.

"Do you see any taxicabs?"

"Why, no!" Ann exclaimed. "But—why aren't there any?"

"Why do you think I went to all the trouble and expense of bringing my car from England? Most taxicabs in Germany have been requisitioned by the *Wehrmacht.*"

"What's *Wehrmacht?*"

"It means *army, military forces.* It's the most popular word in the language in Germany nowadays."

Uncle Dick had rented a small furnished apartment not far from the center of Berlin. He took his responsibility for "polishing up her German" very seriously and was constantly sending her out to buy their food, or odds and ends, a newspaper, magazines, pipe tobacco, candy. "The best way for you to learn German is to speak to people. Never mind if you only know a few words today; tomorrow you'll know more," he would say.

Ann found that he was right. Quite soon she had begun to understand the gist of almost anything that people said to her, and with increasing confidence was able to carry on quite lengthy conversations. To be fluent in German had become very important to her because Uncle Dick wanted her to help him with his articles. He was not writing about the political situation in Germany, but about people's domestic life under the Nazi regime. Every day he and Ann drove around Berlin, or took buses, or the subway, or just walked. They went into shops, watched people buy things, and found out prices. They observed which newspapers people read most, and tried to listen to their comments.

In the evenings Uncle Dick typed furiously from his notes, a cup of black coffee at one side of his typewriter, his pipe and an ashtray on the other. When the article was completed, he corrected it in pencil and Ann painstakingly typed it clean the next morning. She soon discovered that while her uncle did not mind her taking an hour to type a page, or making an occasional spelling error, he became very annoyed when she "failed to use her brains," as he put it. "I admit my handwriting is terrible," he would tell her, "but surely your common-sense would make you realize that a pound of beef could not possibly cost 10 pfennigs."

At the end of March, Hitler had unexpectedly arrived in Berlin from Munich. As soon as it became known that he was to attend a performance of *Aïda* at the opera house, Uncle Dick rushed off to see if he could get tickets. He came back almost two hours later, looking battered but triumphant, waving two tickets for the dress circle. Ann could hardly wait for the evening. "Suppose he doesn't come after all?" she asked Uncle Dick anxiously as they took their seats. Uncle Dick answered, "I think he is coming now. Listen to the noise outside."

As soon as Hitler appeared in the imperial box, the audience rose to its feet and volleys of *"Heil Hitler!"* shook the air. Ann stared at the slight figure leaning on the red velvet railing of the box. Hitler did not look impressive. He even looked somewhat ill at ease as he saluted the audience and forced a smile. At the back of the box loomed two guardsmen in black uniform with

Adolph Hitler embroidered in silver on one sleeve. The lights dimmed at last, and Ann sat down feeling disappointed.

"But there is really nothing wrong with the Nazi regime," she had said that same evening, when she and Uncle Dick had come back from the opera and were having a cup of tea in the small kitchen. "People have nice houses or apartments, gardens, orchards. The shops are loaded with goods, and just look how clean everything is. Not a shred of paper in the streets."

Uncle Dick, sitting awkwardly on a high-backed wooden chair, his long legs stretched out in front of him, frowned. "You talk like a tourist with a guidebook in one hand and a camera in the other," he told Ann. "Many German people are clean and thrifty and like gardens, like many English people. The Nazi regime has nothing to do with it. True, there is less unemployment now, but wages are low, and yes, the shops are loaded, but the products are not of good quality and prices are high. You should know all this after typing my articles. So don't imagine Hitler the benefactor of this country. But don't ask me how he's managed to get Germany in the palm of his hand because I don't know the answer. Maybe it's because the German people were tired and dispirited after losing the war in 1918, have lived through a revolution and economic depression since, and now Hitler makes them feel that they are rich and powerful again. But I don't feel too sure of this explanation. All I can say for certain is that I'm afraid, not only for you and myself, or even for England, but for the whole world."

Ann had sat quietly, listening and clasping her teacup with both hands because its warmth was comforting. She had never heard Uncle Dick talk like this.

He paused and said pensively, "It might be wiser to cut short our stay here. We'll see. . . ."

But they had stayed on after all, and Ann loved every minute. When hot weather came they began to take long drives into the countryside. Sometimes they ate in small inns; sometimes they brought a picnic lunch and chose some pleasant scenic spot in which to eat.

All the same, as the weeks went by, Ann began to realize that the atmosphere around them was somehow changing; something menacing seemed to hover in the air. More and more tanks, barely camouflaged now, moved along the Berlin streets. People speaking English drew unpleasant glances, sometimes even abusive comments. Tourists looked uneasy. The Germans themselves seemed changed. The crowds in cafés, in the theatres, in the streets, looked excited, tense, almost feverish. Ann began to notice that most people gave a quick glance around before speaking to anyone. When she mentioned this to Uncle Dick he smiled grimly. "No, it's not your imagination," he told her. "It's what is known more and more as *der Deutsche Blick*. People realize there are spies around and that every word against Hitler is reported to the Gestapo. You know what that means, don't you? The German Secret Police. People are getting their first taste of what Naziism is really like, but it's too late to shake off the yoke. They have been trained to wear it only too well."

Often they listened on the radio to Hitler shouting deliriously, the same words coming again and again: *Opfer! Kampf! Rasse!* Sacrifice! Battle! Race! In spite of herself Ann could feel the persuasive power of that emotion-charged voice.

Sometimes Uncle Dick would suddenly turn off the

radio, stuff his pipe, and take a long pull. "Hitler is getting the country ready," he would remark. "People believe every word he says. They are in a trance now; soon they will be in a frenzy."

"Suppose there is a war and we're still here in Germany," Ann had asked once. "What would happen to us?"

"We'd be interned, most likely," Uncle Dick had answered, and added quickly, "Don't look so alarmed. If the political news gets too bad, we'll simply clear out and head for home."

In the middle of September Uncle Dick handed her his last article to type and announced that they would be be leaving. "I know your term starts next week," he told her, "and we *should* go straight back, but I think you ought to see a bit more of Germany. It may be the last chance for a very long time!" He unfolded a road map and began to trace out a route. "We'll visit Leipzig, Dresden, Frankfurt on Main, push on to Cologne, and take a boat from Hamburg home, making a giant circle. On the way we'll have a look at all the castles and famous gardens and museums and anything else we can find in the guidebook."

Leipzig . . . Dresden . . . Ann felt spellbound by the very names of the towns Uncle Dick was pointing out. The threat of war seemed very far away. Or did it?

They left Berlin in the rain but the bad weather lasted only a few hours. Soon the roads were dry again and the mellow autumn days seemed even more radiant than those of summer. Uncle Dick kept his word and they visited every interesting sight, sometimes spending several days in one town. Ann went to bed each night wishing the morning would come soon.

They drove into Frankfurt at about five in the afternoon. The newspaper boys were rushing along the streets, waving the evening editions and shouting, "Britain and Germany sign accord!"

Uncle Dick stopped the car and, leaning out of the window, bought a paper. Huge type was splashed across the front page. *We regard the agreement signed on September 30th as symbolic of the desire of our two peoples never to go to war with one another again,* signed *Adolph Hitler* and *Neville Chamberlain.*

Ann felt as though a weight had been lifted from her spirits. War was not coming after all and there was no need to feel apprehensive about staying on in Germany. Now she wished they would never have to go home. She was surprised to see that Uncle Dick was looking grave. "Isn't it . . . good news?" she asked, puzzled, but all he said was, "It buys us a little time, at any rate."

They went sightseeing next day, wandering through the old part of Frankfurt, getting lost in the maze of narrow streets lined with houses that seemed to have come straight from the Grimms' fairy stories. Ann wanted to come back next morning but Uncle Dick persuaded her to see the Palmgarten instead. She agreed and was not sorry. It was like walking in a tropical forest, yet all under glass.

It was almost noon when they came out and got into the car. "Shall we have lunch in Old Frankfurt?" Uncle Dick suggested. "I noticed a nice looking restaurant near the Rathaus. Let's hope we can find it again. I should have asked directions from that man at the gate. Never mind, we can turn into this street on the right and see where it takes us."

"I don't care where it takes us. Everything is so fascinating," Ann answered.

"Yes, Frankfurt is fascinating. The whole of Germany is fascinating, but it's becoming uncomfortable. Just as well we're leaving."

And at that moment they saw the truck coming toward them. It veered, and suddenly loomed above them . . .

3

The House in Mylius Strasse

Once the circle of memories was complete, Ann found herself feeling stronger and distinctly more cheerful. The day soon came when Doctor Fromm said that she could go downstairs.

Uncle Dick had apparently arranged for their hotel to send their luggage to Frau Meixner's. Ann was glad to have her own clothes hanging in the old oaken wardrobe, for she certainly did not intend to go downstairs for the first time wearing a bathrobe. Taking out a blue dress that buttoned in front from top to bottom, she put it on, not without wincing. She would have to wear this dress solidly for the next few days because her shoulder was still too painful to allow her to raise her arm. It did not matter. The most important thing was that she would be leaving the green-striped room for the first time, and, even better, Doctor Fromm had said she would be able to talk to Uncle Dick on the telephone.

She was sitting in the big oak chair, finishing her breakfast coffee, when the door opened a crack to reveal a pair of blue eyes, full of curiosity, staring at her from a freckled face topped by red hair clipped so close the skin showed through. Ann realized this must be Frau Meixner's son, Peter.

Taken by surprise, she choked on her coffee and made a muffled sound that was evidently interpreted by Peter as an invitation to come in. He pushed the door open and entered.

Ann immediately recognized the uniform of *Pimfe,* the youngest division of Hitler's Youth Movement. Peter was clad in the regulation brown shirt and brown shorts, knee-length brown stockings and sturdy ankle-high shoes. Around his neck was a triangular kerchief with little straps at the ends, tied into a knot. Before Ann had time to say anything, he suddenly raised his right hand and said, *"Heil Hitler!"*

"Er . . ." Ann muttered, wondering whether he would insist on her saying, "Heil Hitler," too. But Peter did not wait for a greeting. Edging his way to the table bearing the remains of her breakfast, he pointed at the two buttered rolls in the bread basket. "You are not going to eat them?" he asked hopefully.

Ann shook her head and the rolls vanished in a minute. Taking two lumps of sugar out of the sugar bowl, Peter popped them into his mouth, shook the empty milk jug, and put it down regretfully.

"Didn't you have breakfast?" Ann asked, amused.

"Ya," Peter admitted, "but I need more food. One al-

24

ways needs food when one does a lot of marching and exercising. Max Schwamm, our group fuhrer, says we must do the drill over and over again until we do it perfectly."

Peter was speaking with deep respect. He even threw back his shoulders as if standing at attention.

Suppressing a smile, Ann was just going to ask Peter more about his Hitler's Youth activities, when the boy suddenly leaned over the small table and whispered mysteriously, "Do you know, I've got a secret!"

Ann smiled at him. "Really? How exciting. Would you care to tell me your secret?" she suggested. "I promise not to tell anyone."

The blue eyes searched her face. It was clear that Peter was longing to part with his secret. "Come on!" Ann urged.

But Peter's mouth was already closed in a tight line. "Can't. I swore on the holy book not to tell."

His tone was almost as reverent as when he had spoken about his group fuhrer. He pocketed another lump of sugar and, muttering, "I must be going," walked to the door.

"Wait!" Ann called after him, intrigued. "*Who* made you swear on the holy book? Your friends? Max Schwamm?"

Peter answered curtly, "Mutti," and went out.

"Mutti . . ." Ann repeated to herself. Why on earth would Frau Meixner make her son swear on the Bible . . .? But her thoughts were interrupted and she blushed as Frau Meixner entered the room to clear the table.

"I will come to help you downstairs, Fraulein Anna," Frau Meixner said beaming. "The doctor is coming soon

25

and he will let you speak on the telephone to your Herr oncle."

Frau Meixner's kitchen was big and sunny, with bright yellow walls and flowers in pots on the windowsill. Across the tiny hall was the parlor, dark and a little musty, with heavy furniture upholstered in red plush, and an upright piano that stood between the two windows. There was an enormous vase of wax flowers and a big china gnome holding a candelabra on the round table. Like Ann's room above, the parlor overlooked the street, but the kitchen windows gave onto a small back garden. Not that there was much to be seen: just a few trees, a flowerbed with a bright ball in the middle, and a clothes line. It was a sunny day, but the sky looked pale and far away. Ann's eye fell on a calendar on the wall. She read, *Sonntag, Oktober 24.* No wonder the sky looked almost wintry. Sunday . . . that was why Peter was at home. And she had felt sure it was Friday. Was she losing track of time? She longed to hear Uncle Dick's voice and hoped the doctor would come soon.

He arrived a few minutes later, told Ann she looked fine, and phoned the hospital. The telephone was in the parlor and placed so high on the wall that Ann had to stand on tiptoe to reach it.

She had expected Uncle Dick to sound weak and ill, but his voice was as brisk as usual and he only complained about being confined to his hospital room. "It's driving me insane, just lying here, twiddling my thumbs," he told Ann. "The doctor assures me I'll be all right in about a month's time. A month! That means we'll be stuck here in Frankfurt till the end of November. Still, I suppose it could be much worse. Just you sit tight where you are and do whatever the doctor tells you.

26

I've sent your Frau Meixner a check for your keep, so don't imagine yourself an orphan in the storm. The car is being repaired. By the way, was all the luggage sent over from the hotel? Did you check it, now that you are feeling better? There should be four suitcases and a black briefcase."

"I *think* everything is here," Ann answered doubtfully. "Frau Meixner had all the luggage put into a cupboard in my room, but . . . but I didn't really count it."

Uncle Dick sounded displeased. "What do you mean, you *think?* Make sure as soon as you are back upstairs. All my contracts and some material for articles are in that briefcase. Can't I rely on you for a simple thing like that?"

"I . . . I'm *almost sure.*" Ann gulped, doing her best to keep her voice firm. Uncle Dick relented. "It's all right. I didn't mean to badger you. Never mind the luggage, just get well. I'll call you tomorrow, now that you can get to the telephone."

The end of the conversation cheered Ann up and when Frau Meixner assured her that there were indeed four suitcases *and* a briefcase, she felt quite lighthearted. "Could I go outside just for a second?" she begged the doctor.

"*Ach nein,* Fraulein Anna!" Frau Meixner exclaimed and Doctor Fromm agreed with her. "Tomorrow," he told Ann. "Not everything at once. But you can stay downstairs for lunch. I am invited too, today, if my rounds will permit it."

To Ann's pleasure, they did. Doctor Fromm returned at lunchtime and they sat down together in the sunny kitchen. It was certainly much pleasanter to eat at a proper table in this cheerful room than off a tray in soli-

27

tary state upstairs. Ann was just thinking that Frau Meixner's veal with dumplings was the very best dish she had
ever tasted, when a shuffle of boots sounded outside and
Peter came in. He mumbled a greeting in the doctor's
direction, washed his hands at the sink and sat down at
the table.

Ann expected Frau Meixner to say something, to scold
Peter for being late for lunch, but she only gave him a
rapid glance, heaped a plate with food and put it in front
of him.

Doctor Fromm, who was telling Ann about something
funny that had happened when he was a medical student,
interrupted his story and asked in a jovial tone that somehow did not sound quite natural, "Did you have a good
drill, Peter? You boys never rest, even on weekends!"

Peter looked up from his plate. "We were not drilling
today," he answered, hastily swallowing a mouthful of
dumpling. "We just sat around and talked."

It seemed an innocent enough remark, yet Ann noticed that the doctor and Frau Meixner exchanged anxious glances. Frau Meixner took an apple pudding out of
the oven and set it on the table so jerkily it nearly top-
pled to one side. Doctor Fromm frowned and drummed
on the table. Peter's close-clipped head was bent low over
his plate.

Ann felt ill at ease. Here were two adults, watching an
eleven-year-old boy with something very much like fear.
Peter must have sensed something for he gobbled up his
portion of apple pudding, muttered, "I'm going out on
my bike," and left without waiting for permission.

Frau Meixner looked relieved, but Doctor Fromm remained somber and told Ann somewhat curtly to go upstairs and rest.

She was halfway up the stairs when she happened to glance back and saw something strange. Frau Meixner was heating up the remains of the veal and dumplings.

Why warm up food *after* lunch? Ann tried to puzzle it out as she came to her room, then gave up, telling herself it was none of her business. Kicking off her shoes, she stretched herself on the bed and closed her eyes. Soon, Frau Meixner's steps passed her door and ten minutes later went downstairs again. Ann was not paying any attention. She was thinking how nice it would be to go outdoors tomorrow.

4

Two New Acquaintances

The first day Ann just sat in the garden, breathing the moist autumn air that smelled of decaying leaves. Two days later she was walking briskly round and round the trees and the flower bed, feeling almost completely recovered. Walking was good for her, Doctor Fromm said, so she walked. There was nothing else to do anyway. She wished she had someone of her own age to talk to, but there seemed to be no hope of that.

On the left of Frau Meixner's house was Doctor Fromm's, an exact copy, as was the house beyond. The house on the right, however, was much newer and larger. It occupied the whole corner and was three storeys high. Frau Meixner told Ann that, a few years before, two of the old houses had been pulled down to make way for this building. It contained three apartments, she said, all very luxurious. The entrance was round the corner in Feldberg Strasse. The house had an elevator and even a doorman, Frau Meixner said respectfully.

Ann often scanned the three rows of back windows that overlooked Frau Meixner's garden. Sometimes one opened, but nothing more exciting appeared than a hand shaking a duster or scattering crumbs for the birds. She had almost given up watching when, on the third day, a girl's face looked through the panes of the third-floor corner window. The sun reflecting on the glass made it difficult for Ann to see, but she could make out that the girl was about her own age, dark haired, and wearing something pink.

She was shading her eyes with her hand and looking up, when someone behind her called, "Fraulein Anna!"

Ann turned around. A little figure stood behind the garden gate. It was draped in the folds of a red velvet cloak, and its head, too big in proportion to its short body, was made even bigger by an extraordinary tam-o'-shanter, also of red velvet. From beneath the heat peered a round face with solemn, pale gray eyes almost totally devoid of lashes.

The figure made a slight plunge that was probably meant to be a curtsy and said, *"Guten Morgen,* Fraulein Anna. My name is Minna Fromm. I live next door."

Minna's voice was high-pitched and she enunciated every word very clearly as if she were repeating a lesson learned by heart.

Goodness, Ann thought, this must be the doctor's stepsister. Aloud, she said, "Thank you very much for the cakes. It was very kind of you to make them for me."

Minna nodded solemnly. "I am glad you liked them. I

love to cook. Sister Hanna taught me." Coming closer, she leaned on the gate and said wistfully, "I used to come and help Frau Meixner when she was cooking. Why doesn't she want me to come any more? Is she angry with me? But I have been good."

"Of course she's not angry with you," Ann said reassuringly, though she really had no idea why Minna should not be welcome. "I expect she is . . . too busy for visitors."

Minna did not answer. She just stood with folded hands, looking forlorn. Trying to change the subject, Ann asked quickly, "Can you see that girl in the window? Do you know who she is?"

Minna raised her head. "Yes, I know her. Her name is Eleonore Von Wal-den-fels. She can't walk."

"Can't walk?" Ann echoed. "Is she an invalid?"

"I don't know what that is," Minna answered truthfully. "She just can't walk. She sits in a chair with big wheels. I saw her in the street," she counted on her fingers, "one . . . two times."

Ann wanted to find out more about Eleonore, but Minna was already moving on. "I must go home," she informed Ann, "and finish my book. It is a very good book, *The Princess and the Frog*. My brother gave it to me for my birthday. Have you read it?"

"I think I have," Ann answered just as seriously. "Well, goodbye then."

Minna said, *"Aufwiedersehen,"* and, *"Grussen Sie Frau Meixner,"* very primly and walked away, her cloak swishing around her. From the window above, the girl in pink seemed to watch with interest.

When Ann went inside for lunch, she made a point of repeating to Frau Meixner her conversation with Minna, hoping that the older woman would say, "Of course she must come and cook," but just the opposite happened. Frau Meixner looked worried and exclaimed shrilly, *"Hier darf sie nicht kommen!"* and quickly changed the subject. But she was very ready to talk about Eleonore. Apparently the girl's father, Colonel Von Waldenfels, was a prominent member of the Nazi party in Frankfurt. Eleonore was an only child. About two years ago she had had a terrible accident. She had fallen down a stairwell and had irreparably injured her spine. There was no Frau Von Waldenfels. The colonel was thought to be a widower. There was quite a large staff of servants for just two people: Eleonore's personal maid, another maid for general work, a cook, and a woman who came three times a week for heavy cleaning.

But Ann was interested in Eleonore, not in the servants. "Does she go out often in her wheelchair?" she asked.

Frau Meixner looked surprised. "You mean in the street? Oh, no! Never. She did at first; her governess wheeled her. But I suppose she did not like people staring at her."

How I wish I could talk to her! Ann thought as she went outside the next morning.

Eleonore was at the window again. When she saw Ann she opened it a crack and threw out something white. Ann ran up and caught a small envelope attached to an empty spool. When she glanced up, Eleonore was gesturing at her to read the letter. Ann nodded back and tore the envelope open.

The letter was in English and written on thick, expensive-looking paper with *Eleonore Von Waldenfels* engraved at the top.

33

Dear Ann, it said. *I hope you don't mind my calling you by your first name. Trudi, my maid, found it out for me. She also told me about your accident. You look lonely walking in that small garden and I am very lonely too. Would you come to tea this afternoon about three? We could talk and cheer each other up. It would give me great pleasure. If you can come, please wave. Sincerely, Eleonore Von Waldenfels.*

The letter in her hand, Ann thought swiftly. There was no reason why she should refuse the invitation. Uncle Dick would not mind, and Frau Meixner had spoken of the Von Waldenfels with great respect. Resolutely, she waved her hand and Eleonore answered by thrusting her fingers out through the crack.

It was a windy morning and rather cold. Ann was not surprised when a white-capped maid suddenly appeared from behind Eleonore and closed the window.

Ann thrust the letter into the pocket of her coat and went inside. Feeling pleased and excited, she decided to call the hospital at once and tell Uncle Dick about Eleonore's invitation. He was highly amused. "Well! It sounds as though you are getting in with the cream of Nazi society," he teased. "No harm in your visiting the girl, of course. It will do you good to talk to someone of your own age. Only don't be oversympathetic about her plight. And while you're at it, what about visiting your old uncle on his sick bed? Doctor Fromm reported this morning that you have improved so much you can actually undertake a streetcar ride."

She was going to see Uncle Dick! Ann was so thrilled that she almost forgot about Eleonore, but Uncle Dick reminded her by shouting just before she hung up, "Don't forget to tell Frau Meixner that you are going

34

out, and where. Remember you're under her care."

"Of course I will," Ann assured him. "Not that she will mind."

Unexpectedly, Frau Meixner did mind. "You are going to see those people," she murmured, blinking rapidly and placing a saucepan perilously close to the edge of the stove. "Fraulein Anna, you . . . you are not going to make trouble for me, are you?"

"Why, of course not! How could I!? I don't know what you mean," Ann answered, feeling puzzled and vaguely offended. Frau Meixner muttered something about not meaning anything, but one had to be so careful nowadays. Then she became friendly again and accepted Ann's offer to help with the vegetables. But the atmosphere remained troubled and Ann was glad when, toward noon, Peter arrived home from school.

He stomped into the kitchen looking tired and cross. In one hand he carried a satchel crammed with books, in the other a canvas bag full of groceries. "Here you are!" he announced, slamming the bag down on the nearest chair.

"Careful! You'll break the milk bottles!" Frau Meixner screamed, seizing the bag. "Did you get two as I told you? And the meat?"

"I got everything, but I am not going to do it any more!" Peter grumbled. He stood glaring at the groceries, his feet planted apart, his lower lip stuck out. "I am tired of making up stories about why I can't go home with the other boys. Two of them live just near here and they can't understand why I want to stay behind after school when we could all go together."

"But, Peterchen, the grocer is just across the street from the school and . . ." Frau Meixner began, then looked at Ann and said hastily, "I am afraid lunch will be a little late today, Fraulein Anna. I have to put all these groceries away. If you don't mind . . ."

Ann took the hint. Slowly mounting the staircase—she still did not have enough energy to *run* up—she kept thinking about the scene she had just witnessed. She did not know exactly where Peter's school was, but she knew it must be some distance away because he took the street-car to get there. But even if there was a shop near the school, why was it necessary for Peter to lug groceries all that way when everything could be bought in Feldberg Strasse, around the corner?

She did not ponder long on this subject. After all it did not really concern her and the important thing was to get ready for her visit to Eleonore. She decided to wear the dress Uncle Dick had bought her just before they left Berlin. Made of pale green wool, it was slightly shirred at the shoulders and the flared skirt reached just below the knee. The buttons in front and the belt were of brown leather.

"It makes me feel really grown-up," Ann had said when she was trying it on in the shop, and Uncle Dick had answered, "Well, you *are* growing up . . . I hope!" She had not worn the dress yet because she was keeping it for some special occasion. This was a special occasion.

She was annoyed to find a hole in the heel of her best stockings. Setting her teeth as if for a great ordeal, she threaded a needle and began to draw the edges of the hole together. "Learn to know your limitations and don't attempt something you cannot do," one of the teachers at Rivington had once said, and Ann always remembered these words when faced with sewing.

As she worked, her thoughts drifted back to Frau

Meixner and Peter. What was it that struck her as strange only a couple of days ago? Oh, yes! She remembered now. Frau Meixner had brought home two bags of bread and rolls. The name of the bakery was different on each bag, yet the bread and rolls were almost exactly the same. Ann had not paid much attention at the time, but now she wondered. . . .

"Fraulein Anna, lunch is ready!" Frau Meixner called from downstairs. Ann sighed. No matter how often she asked Frau Meixner to call her just "Anna," it was always "Fraulein Anna," and it sounded so solemn. Should she ask her again? After some rapid thinking, Ann decided to give up. "Fraulein Anna" she would remain till the end of her stay in Mylius Strasse. Hastily snapping the thread, she flung the stocking over the back of a chair.

Lunch did not last long. Peter was completely silent and gobbled his food as if this was his last meal. Frau Meixner looked upset. Ann was only too glad she could use her visit to Eleonore as a pretext to go upstairs to change, as soon as she had finished.

5

Eleonore Von Waldenfels

The lobby of the building where Eleonore lived was small but elegant, with a beige carpet and a group of potted palms in one corner. The uniformed doorman, about whom Frau Meixner had spoken with such awe, directed her to the elevator. A young, sharp-faced maid opened the door of the apartment and conducted Ann to Eleonore's room.

Wishing that her arms and legs had not suddenly become so long and awkward, Ann followed the maid, staring at the big painting of a hunting scene hanging on the wall of the oak-paneled hall. Everything seemed gigantic compared to Frau Meixner's small home: the drawing room with a concert piano, the library whose walls were lined with bookshelves from floor to ceiling.

Eleonore's room was almost as big as the drawing room. Walking across the thick white rug that separated her from the slight figure in the wheelchair, Ann's first thought was: How pretty she is! But not just pretty in an ordinary way. She is like . . . like Tinker Bell in *Peter Pan*.

Eleonore's dark eyes, set wide apart in a saucy, heart-shaped face, watched Ann's progress across the room with barely disguised amusement. She shook back the cloud of fluffy black hair that fell in tendrils down to her shoulders, and said in a lilting voice, "How do you do? I am so glad you could come."

She spoke without a trace of accent and Ann thought: She could go to Rivington Academy, even, and no one would guess she was German.

"Please sit down," Eleonore went on, obviously trying to put her guest at ease. "How do you like my room? Papa had it redecorated for me last spring."

Ann sank with relief onto the cretonne-covered stool by the side of the wheelchair and stared about her. "I think it is just about the most beautiful room I've ever seen!" she said. Eleonore looked pleased.

It was an extraordinarily pretty room. The soft pinks and greens of the wallpaper and curtains were repeated in the upholstery of the white-lacquered furniture, and everything in it had obviously been designed for Eleonore's comfort. The bookcase was large but low, so that one did not have to stand up or stretch in order to get out a book. A tall lamp under a pink shade stood at just the right angle by the wheelchair. There was even a special table that could swing across the lap of the person sitting in the wheelchair, or swing back when no longer needed. The top of the table was shaped like a tray with raised

39

edges so that things could not fall off. It held a half-finished box of chocolates, a puzzle, and a book. *Les Contes de Grand-mère par George Sand,* Ann read on the cover.

"You read French just for pleasure?" she asked with awe. It seemed almost incredible that someone should open a French book without being ordered to do so.

Eleonore shrugged her shoulders indifferently. "I've had foreign governesses all my life. Sometimes two, a French and an English one. It is only for the last couple of months that I've had no one. *La situation politique n'est pas sure,*" she mimicked in French. "I liked Miss Mannering the best. She was English. She spent almost five years with me. After she left, about a year ago, Papa got me a French one, Mademoiselle Suchard. *She* stayed several months, but I finally got rid of her."

"You did?" Ann gasped, impressed by this offhand way of settling the matter. "Why? Didn't you like her?"

"Oh, I liked her well enough at first, but then something happened." Eleonore's face darkened and her voice became hard and brittle. "She was talking on the telephone one day and she did not know I'd had Trudi wheel me into the library. I could hear every word. She was telling someone how she was looking forward to the day she would have enough money saved to return to France, get married, and not have to teach 'that spoiled little Boche' any more. Do you know what 'Boche' means? That is what French people call Germans when they want to show how they despise them. As soon as Papa came home I told him about it. He discharged her at once, only he was too nice about it. He paid her a month's salary in advance and took her to the station in his car."

40

"There are no taxis," Ann ventured timidly.

"All the better," Eleonore retorted. "She should have been made to carry her suitcases on her back. If I'd had my way, I'd have had her things thrown out onto the pavement, but when I told Papa, he only laughed and told me to hold onto my temper."

Eleonore's face had changed. It had become older and pinched, and her thin hands clutched at the arms of her chair. Ann said nothing, frightened a little by the icicles in Eleonore's voice and eyes.

It was Eleonore herself who changed the subject. "That's a pretty dress," she remarked. "Pale green goes well with your coloring."

Ann was pleased. "That's just what my Uncle Dick said. I have a striped one he bought me, as well, a very nice one."

Eleonore's eyebrows went up slightly. "Your uncle chooses your clothes? *I* have been choosing my own clothes since I was ten. I love blue, but of course pink suits me better." Eleonore smoothed her pink silk wrapper. "Papa is fair-haired, but I take after my mother. She is an Italian."

"Oh . . . I thought your mother . . ." Ann began and bit her tongue.

Eleonore's face darkened again. "You thought my mother was dead, didn't you? Well, she is not, at least I don't think so. She simply packed and left, five years ago. Why do you stare at me like that? I am not inventing it. I was old enough to remember."

Looking straight in front of her, Eleonore hurried on, gasping a little as if she were out of breath. "I remember *everything*. It was December 1933, just before the New Year. I was having a nap and Papa was at the barracks.

Miss Mannering told me afterward that my mother came into my room and kissed me while I slept. I don't care if she did. Anyway, when Papa came home my mother was gone . . . for good. I heard the maids say that she had left a letter for Papa. I don't know what she wrote in it, but I can guess. There was a girl at school. Hildegarde something-or-other. We sat at the same desk. She told me once that *her* mother left because she liked another man better than her husband, Hildegarde's father, I mean. I think that my mother loved another man better than she did Papa and . . . and *I* did not matter. Papa tried to make me believe that she was sick and did not know what she was doing. I pretended I swallowed the story, but . . ."

Eleonore turned her head away and the dark cloud of her hair hid her face.

Before Ann could decide whether she should say something or simply keep quiet because she did not really know what to say, the maid, Trudi, appeared with a tea tray. Eleonore shook back her hair and became a gay hostess again.

The piles of small sandwiches and fancy cakes grew considerably smaller as the two girls ate and talked. There were rows of English books in Eleonore's bookcase. Ann discovered that her new friend shared her tastes in authors. They were in the middle of a heated discussion of whether Angela Brazil's school stories were too old-fashioned or not, when Ann happened to glance at her wristwatch. Almost four thirty! "I must go," she said regretfully. "Frau Meixner is probably wondering what has happened to me."

At the mention of Frau Meixner's name, a flicker passed in Eleonore's dark eyes. Leaning forward, she whispered, "Tell me, now we are friends: who is it lives in the attic?"

"In the attic?" Ann was totally taken aback. "You mean the attic in Frau Meixner's house? Why, no one. We all sleep on the second floor. Peter's room is next to his mother's and mine is across the landing."

"Peter?" Eleonore frowned. "Is that the little freckled boy? I know him by sight. No, it could not be his shadow. He is too short."

As Ann only blinked and said nothing, Eleonore went on, "I *know* someone lives in that attic. There is a thick curtain in the window and I suppose no one can see any light from *below*, but if one looks from *above*, a sliver of light shows. And last night, no, the night before, I saw a shadow. It was blurred, but it was certainly too tall for that boy."

Ann listened, feeling at first surprised, then more and more irritated. When Eleonore paused, she said sharply, "No one lives in the attic. The shadow you saw was probably Frau Meixner rummaging in some old trunk."

"All right," Eleonore conceded, "let's suppose it *was* Frau Meixner that one time, but the light has been on every night for about two months. Surely, your landlady wouldn't be rummaging in old trunks *every* night."

"How do you know the light has been on every night?" Ann wanted to know. "Don't you sleep?"

Eleonore rubbed her forehead with a tired gesture. "Very badly. It takes me a long time to doze off and then I wake up frequently. Miss Mannering used to make a sort of *tisane* that made me all drowsy and comfortable. It was tea and honey and some herbs. But since she left, no one has bothered about whether I sleep or not. So I just wait until it is all quiet and then I get out of bed and sit

43

by the window, or just walk around the room."

"*Walk!*" Ann exclaimed.

Eleonore looked at her defiantly. "Yes, *walk*. You heard me right. My legs are in order. I smashed my back and my left hip in that accident."

"But then why, *why*," Ann asked wildly, "are you sitting in that wheelchair?"

"Why, *why?*" Eleonore imitated her. "Because I cannot keep my back straight. I hobble along all bent, no, worse: *lopsided*. I cannot bear to see myself walk, or let other people see me."

Ann felt desperately sorry for Eleonore. Before she could think of the right thing to say, Eleonore abruptly switched the conversation back to the attic. "I found Mother's old opera glasses," she announced, "and tonight I'm going to have a good look. My bedroom windows overlook your backyard too," she gestured toward the door at the other end of the room. "Are you sure you haven't any clue? I thought you might know something since you live in that house."

Something flared up inside Ann. "Is that why you invited me?" she asked, looking Eleonore full in the face. "You didn't really want to make friends. You just planned to use me for spying on Frau Meixner."

"Oh, *no!*" The words came out spontaneously and some instinct told Ann she could believe them.

"I didn't mean it at all like that," Eleonore pleaded. "I simply thought it would be fun if we both tried to solve the mystery, like in one of those books. The curtain is always down in the daytime, so there must be something strange going on. You may not understand it, but I enjoy, yes, *enjoy* watching that attic window. It gives me something to look forward to every night. You can run and play games; why can't I play a game of my own?"

Once again, Ann felt sorry for the crippled girl. "I see what you mean," she said, "but really there is nothing. Maybe there is no light at all, just a reflection in the windowpane."

"Maybe," Eleonore agreed.

Ann realized Eleonore did not believe her, but wanted desperately for them to part friends. It must be dreadfully lonely, never going out, and being taught by governesses. It almost excused making up fantasies about Frau Meixner's attic. Almost.

It was cold and dark in the street. The wind swept leaves across the pavement and twirled the long skirts of a nun walking in front of Ann. Rain hung in the air.

She could not make up her mind about Eleonore. Did she like her or didn't she? And more immediately: should she tell Frau Meixner about Eleonore watching the attic? It was too fantastic, the idea of someone living secretly up there, but she could not help remembering Frau Meixner heating up the food after the meal . . . the odd duplication of the bag of rolls . . .

She shook her head impatiently and shifted the loan of books Eleonore had insisted on lending her in token of their meeting soon again. Eleonore's fantasy must be catching. And it *was* just a fantasy: the idle imaginings of a bored and lonely girl trying to fill the empty hours of the night.

All the same, by the time Ann reached the front door of Frau Meixner's house, she had resolved to say nothing about it.

45

6

The Discovery

The visit to Uncle Dick at the hospital was not a great success. Ann had hoped to have a long chatty hour telling him everything about Frau Meixner and Minna Fromm and Peter and Eleonore, and she decided she would tell him also about Eleonore's wild ideas about someone in the attic and ask him what he thought. But she missed the streetcar to the hospital and another did not come for ages, so visiting hours were half over when she finally rushed up the steps and presented herself at the reception desk.

Then, she wasn't prepared to find Uncle Dick all strung up under traction. He laughed when he saw her face, and some of the accustomed edge came into his voice as he denounced those aspects of the nursing rou-

tine which he found particularly oppressive to his free
spirit, but from time to time, despite his jokes, his
crooked eyebrows met as if he were in pain. Clearly he
was not much interested in hearing about the Meixner
household or Ann's new friend, and he made no attempt
to detain her when Doctor Fromm came to collect her at
the end of visiting hours.

"Do not think your uncle is in any danger," Doctor
Fromm comforted Ann as they walked down the corridor
together. "Traction cases always look very frightening, but
in fact we are pleased with Herr Lindsay's progress. The
leg is coming along famously, and though that back is
giving him a bit of pain, I'm afraid, it will clear with the
weather. You'll see."

Ann was grateful to the doctor for being so kind, but
she felt downhearted and tired, herself, after her first real
outing. She had also discovered that she was afraid of
cars. As she walked to the streetcar stop, it seemed to her
that every passing car was rushing straight at her. It was a
relief to get back to Mylius Strasse.

She had barely entered the house when she heard
voices coming from the kitchen. *"Nein, nein und nein!"*
Frau Meixner was screaming, and Peter's piercing treble
answered something.

Trying to step as lightly as possible, Ann ran past the
kitchen door and up the stairs. Behind her Peter shrilled,
"Why can't I have my friends here for the monthly meeting? It is my turn! *Warum nicht?"*

"You know very well why not!" his mother's voice rose
higher with each word.

Goodness, what a row! Ann thought, thankfully reaching her room.

It seemed, however, that after all the arguments, Frau

47

Meixner had given in. The next afternoon the kitchen table was covered with a blue checked cloth, crackling with starch. On one end stood a jug full of milk surrounded by mugs and glasses, and on the other a basket piled with gingerbread, and a dish of apples.

Peter collected chairs from all over the house and announced that his *Kamaraden* were going to arrive at three. Frau Meixner only snorted in response. But she did not retire to her room as Ann expected she would. As soon as the first pair of hobnailed shoes clattered up the front steps, she planted herself on the landing and sat there on an uncomfortable three-legged stool, knitting all through the meeting.

Ann deliberated for a few minutes whether she should keep Frau Meixner company or go up to her room and read, but the prospect of Eleonore's books proved too tempting. She was soon stretched full length on the faded carpet, her mind far away from Mylius Strasse. She did not even hear the voices, laughter, and singing that floated from the kitchen.

It was almost five by the time she went downstairs. The meeting was over; only the chairs were still scattered all over the room. Peter, his mother's apron around his middle, was glumly washing glasses at the sink.

At the sound of Ann's footsteps, Frau Meixner rushed out of the living room. "Oh, Fraulein Anna. I have been talking on the telephone and I want to ask you . . ." She rattled on and Ann did her best to follow, wishing Frau Meixner would sometimes slow down a little. But she got the gist of it. Peter's godmother, who lived in Offenbach-on-Main, was celebrating her golden wedding and she had invited Frau Meixner and Peter to dinner.

"She is an elderly lady and very frail," Frau Meixner

explained to Ann. "She seldom goes out of the house, but she has many friends and they are all coming to help her celebrate. Would you mind very much staying in the house alone tomorrow afternoon, Fraulein Anna? Dinner will be early and we should be back by eight. I will prepare your supper and leave it in the oven. But no, I can't leave you like that! I am going to say we cannot go."

"Oh, please don't do that!" Ann exclaimed. "Of course you must go, Frau Meixner. I don't mind staying alone, honestly. I can take care of myself."

"Danke, danke schon," Frau Meixner murmured and rushed back to the telephone.

"I can take care of myself." Ann repeated the words for her own benefit as she stood on the front steps waving goodbye to Frau Meixner and Peter.

The house felt strange when she went inside. For a second she felt almost sorry she had not taken Frau Meixner at her word when the older woman murmured something about, "Frau Lemke would not mind your joining us, Fraulein Anna."

Ann had quickly answered, "Thank you, but I have letters to write." She knew she would feel out of place among all those strangers and probably be bored to death as well. From what Frau Meixner told her, she gathered that Offenbach was a small town just outside Frankfurt where there were big leather goods factories. It did not sound very exciting. Besides, I *do* have letters to write, she reminded herself and went upstairs to her room. As she reached the landing, she stopped and looked thoughtfully at the narrow flight of steps leading to the attic. This was her chance to prove to Eleonore that there was no one hiding under the rafters. She could not see the attic

49

door but it was unlikely to be locked. She put her foot on the first step, then drew it back. No, she was not going to spy on Frau Meixner. Let Eleonore imagine things, if it amused her.

Entering her room, Ann settled herself to write to her two best friends. *Dear Joan and Muriel,* she wrote. *You are probably wondering where I am and what I'm doing. You'll never believe it when I tell you! What happened was this. . . .*

Usually, Ann did not much care for writing letters, but it was fun to describe the accident and her life in Mylius Strasse. She became so carried away that after finishing the letter she wrote postcards to most of her old classmates at Rivington. When she addressed the last card, she rose, stretched herself, and went to the window. It was quite dark outside. Long streaks of rain flashed past the street light.

"B-r-r . . ." Ann muttered, backing away from the chilly draft that came from underneath the window. Never mind, she would give herself a treat. She would eat her supper and read at the same time. Tucking her book under her arm, she ran downstairs.

A heatproof plate holding slices of roast beef and vegetables was in the oven. Ann carried it to the table and propped her book against a vase filled with red-gold autumn leaves. Now for some milk and she would be quite comfortable.

There was almost no milk left in the bottle after Ann had poured herself a glass, but there was another full one. Or *was* there? She peered into the depths of the larder. The bottle was gone and so were the big bowl of chicken and noodle soup and a plate of stewed apples. Could it be that Frau Meixner had taken all that food to Offenbach as her contribution to the feast? Standing by the larder, Ann tried to visualize Frau Meixner and Peter as they were leaving the house. Frau Meixner was carrying a flat carton with a cake she had baked and Peter had a bowl of some special salad tied in a napkin. They could not have possibly carried anything else.

Sitting down at the table, Ann forced herself to eat. She did not even glance at the opened book. Question after question popped into her head and as she found the answers, everything began to fit like a giant puzzle.

Why was Peter made to shop for groceries in a different neighborhood? Because his mother did not want to attract the attention of the local tradesmen by buying too many groceries. Why had Frau Meixner spent the morning fussing around the stove and yet the larder was empty? Because she was feeding someone.

Jumping up, Ann ran to the breadbox standing on a shelf and opened it. Surely they could not have eaten all that bread at breakfast! And the oranges? There were four in the wicker basket, now only two remained.

But neither Frau Meixner nor Peter had stepped out of the house until they left for Offenbach. Peter had not even gone to school. He was excused for the day. That meant . . . that could mean only one thing . . . whoever Frau Meixner was feeding *was in the house.*

Ann stood still, clutching the back of a chair. The house had suddenly become full of sounds she had never noticed before. The ticking of the moon-faced kitchen clock, the dripping of the faucet, the swish of the rain outside, everything sounded too loud, too close, vaguely menacing. It's because I am all alone, she thought and checked herself. She was not really alone, someone else was listening too, listening to *her.* But where? She knew

51

there was nothing in the cellar except the furnace and a pile of coal. So it had to be the attic.

With a sudden surge of desperate courage, Ann ran up the staircase. Whatever happened would be better than not knowing. She reached the attic door and listened. It seemed to her that she heard a faint intake of breath, but she could not be sure. Setting her teeth, she grasped the doorknob. It would not turn. The door was locked securely.

Holding tight to the banisters because her knees were trembling, Ann retraced her steps. She was on the landing when the telephone began to ring downstairs. The sound jarred her nerves so violently that she gave a slight scream. But at the same time it calmed her, made her realize she was not cut off from the rest of the world. Racing down, two steps at a time, she rushed into the parlor and snatched up the receiver. "Hello," she said breathlessly.

"Hello, Ann," Uncle Dick's voice came cheerfully down the wire. Suddenly, it changed and he asked sharply, "Why do you sound so out of breath? Anything wrong?"

Ann's fingers tightened around the receiver. What a relief it would be to shout, "Everything is wrong! I am alone and frightened to death and there is someone hiding in the attic." But she could not do it. First, it was not her secret, but Frau Meixner's; second, there was nothing Uncle Dick could do about it except be worried.

"I ran down the stairs," she answered, trying to sound nonchalant. "There is no one else in the house to answer the phone."

"Your Frau Meixner ought to have an extension upstairs," Uncle Dick grumbled. "However, I suppose a lodger with a hospital-bound uncle doesn't happen every day of the week so it would scarcely be worth it. The good lady can be pardoned. I rang to ask how you are feeling. I'm afraid I was pretty poor company, day before yesterday. This back thing can be the very devil. But if you're feeling up to it, I'd love another visit. Running down the stairs sounds like a fairly full recovery to me, so you've not got much excuse, Niece, Ward, and Only Living Relative!"

Ann promised that she would come the next day, and after some cheerful remarks about feeling like a trussed turkey, which indicated that Uncle Dick's spirits had definitely risen, he rang off.

She stared at the telephone, and was seized with a wild desire to call Uncle Dick back under some pretext—any pretext—just for the comfort of hearing his voice.

To avoid temptation, she turned her back on the instrument and went to look at the weather. The rain had changed to sleet. The passing cars had their windshields covered with ice, the pavements glistened white. Ann started. Behind her, the telephone was ringing again.

This time it was Frau Meixner. Almost crying, she told Ann that she and Peter had waited almost an hour at the station until it was announced on the loudspeaker that trains between Offenbach and Frankfurt would not be running for the rest of the night. She and Peter had no choice but to go back to Frau Lemke's and sleep there. "I am so sorry to leave you all by yourself, Fraulein Anna," Frau Meixner lamented. "We will be back as soon as the trains are running tomorrow morning. Please make sure the doors are locked and the lights turned out. Electricity is so dear . . ."

It seemed ridiculous to confront Frau Meixner with the

story about the attic on the telephone. Besides, Ann felt so tired she was not even afraid any more. She simply promised to see to the doors and lights and was actually glad when Frau Meixner hung up with a last "Oh, *mein Gott!*"

Her mind a blank, her head aching, Ann washed her plate and glass, checked the doors and turned out all the lights. Walking upstairs in the dark was creepy, but it was only when she reached her room and thought of the long night ahead that a cold fear gripped her again.

Locking her door securely, she put on her bathrobe and stretched on the bed. It was safer not to go to sleep, she decided, but already her eyes were beginning to close.

Dozing off and waking up again. . . . The hours dragged on and on. She had left her bedside lamp alight; that was her only comfort. It was about eleven thirty when it seemed to her that the front door opened and closed. Sitting up in bed she listened intently. No, everything was quiet. How early would Frau Meixner and Peter arrive? Seven, eight? It meant many more hours. Ann started to work out how many exactly, and fell asleep.

7

In the Attic

She woke up because somewhere in the house a child was crying. It was a high-pitched, desperate crying, as if the child were struggling for breath.

Sitting up in bed, Ann listened. There could be no doubt about it, the crying was coming from the attic. There was no time to think. The child needed help, or it would not cry like that.

Ann got up, put on her slippers and tightened the belt of her bathrobe. The crying was getting more and more frantic. She opened her door and peered out onto the landing. The house was in total darkness, but from upstairs the crying now swelled to a long anguished wail.

She stumbled up the short flight of steps and had her hand on the attic doorknob when she remembered the door was locked and she could not possibly get in. I *must,* she thought wildly, and flung herself against the door. It opened wide, almost sending her headlong onto the floor.

Ann steadied herself and saw that she had narrowly missed falling into a large basin of water placed near the door. Standing in the water was a china candlestick holding a stub of a candle. By its flickering light, she could see a bed against the wall under the slanted roof and, huddled on the bed, a little girl of about five or six. The child had stopped crying at Ann's entrance and only whimpered and hiccuped, staring at her with frightened dark eyes.

"Oh, you poor little thing!" Ann exclaimed. Sitting down on the bed, she drew the child into her arms. "There, there," she crooned, patting the mop of tightly waving black curls and murmuring every soothing word in English and German that came into her mind.

It seemed a little strange that after several minutes, the child still did not say a word. She was trembling less and her small hands were not plucking at Ann so frantically, but there was not a sound from her.

Pins and needles began to prick Ann's legs. She shifted her position slightly and the child looked up. Her eyes examined Ann's face and her lips opened, but only a queer little sound escaped.

What is the matter with her? Ann wondered. Could she be . . .

Suddenly she stiffened and clasped the child tighter. Someone was coming up the stairs.

Ann's eyes darted to the door. If she could only make a dash for her room. . . . But she knew only too well that she could not run with the child in her arms. It was too late anyway. The steps, stealthy at first, were now running swiftly and firmly up the steps. The intruder was not bothering any more to make a secret of his arrival.

Ann leaned forward, blew out the candle and shrank into the shadows. Her heart was pounding at her ribs and her throat was dry. The steps reached the landing and a slender silhouette appeared in the attic doorway. A flashlight's beam swept across the walls, picked out Ann and the little girl and held them in the bright circle of light. A girlish voice exclaimed in German, "Oh, you have found us after all!"

The deep dismay in the tone of the speaker made Ann feel guilty. She blurted out, "I'm so sorry, I did not mean to intrude, but the child was crying so dreadfully."

"Rachel!" The dim figure made a step forward, but the little girl had already wriggled out of Ann's arms and rushed to the speaker. The beam of light shifted and Ann saw that the child was clasping the knees of a girl who looked about fourteen or fifteen. She was clad in a raincoat and had a scarf on her head. "No, no," she said, pushing the child gently away from her. "Don't come so close, Rachel. I'm all wet, you will catch cold. Rachel, *please* let me go. I want to turn on the light."

A switch clicked and a low lamp standing on a small table lit up. Not that it gave much light because in addition to the heavy lampshade it was covered by a makeshift screen made of two pieces of cardboard. But it was enough for Ann to see more of the girl who was pulling off her wet coat. She was tall and very thin with long blonde hair tied back. As the coat came off, Ann noticed that the girl had on a cotton dress. At least the bottom looked like a blue and white dotted cotton. The top was hidden by a gray pullover that hung in folds over the narrow shoulders.

57

Rachel still did not say a word. She was only uttering little joyous sounds and jumping up and down, the flashlight in her hand. The older girl exclaimed, "Darling, don't! Suppose it shows through the curtain!" She took the flashlight away, put it on the table and sat down beside Ann. "I suppose you will want to know all about us, now that you have found our hiding place," she said bitterly.

"You don't have to," Ann answered hastily. "You really don't." But the girl went on as if she did not hear. "I *knew* you would find us one day. I was terrified when Frau Meixner took you in, but Doctor Fromm explained to me that Frau Meixner needed money now that she had two more people to feed, and that your uncle was going to pay for your keep. Well . . . he did not put it exactly like that, but that's what he meant. We always walked in our stockinged feet, so you would not hear us, and I kept Rachel as quiet as possible. It is not difficult. She is always drowsy, probably because she does not get any fresh air." She glanced at the little girl, nestled against her shoulder, and sighed. "I never thought she would wake up and scream tonight. She was sleeping so soundly when I left and I arranged a night-light for her. I hated to leave her alone, but I just had to go out, and with Frau Meixner away it seemed the right time."

"But I'm not going to tell anyone about your hiding here," Ann insisted. "Honestly." Then she added, "I don't even know *why* you are hiding."

The girl looked incredulous. "Haven't you guessed that we are Jewish?"

As Ann only looked blank, she went on impatiently, "Who else would have a reason for hiding? Frau Meixner said you had been living in Germany for several months. Surely, you must know what it is to be Jewish here."

Ann did not answer immediately. She was thinking back, remembering the day she had seen a statue in a public park in Berlin. It represented a man about to crush a serpent's head with a hammer. The inscription read, *There can be no health for the German people until the Jews are routed out.*

"Why do they hate the Jews so much?" she had asked Uncle Dick and he answered, "Because someone has to be blamed for Germany losing the war, for the bad economic situation, for lack of employment, and the Jewish people make a handy scapegoat. Hitler realizes it only too well and he is using every pretext to fan the hate." Then he explained that in 1935 new regulations concerning Jews had been issued by the government. They were known as the "Nuremberg Laws." According to those laws, the Jews were no longer German citizens and had no right to display the German flag. They were forbidden to marry "Aryans" and could not keep a German servant younger than forty-five years of age. Little by little they were dismissed from public office jobs and from private ones too. They could only shop at certain hours of the day and not at every shop. When they walked along the streets they had to carry a small identification card marked *Jew* in their hand, so that it could be easily seen.

At the time, Ann was impressed and indignant, but outside of the slogans everywhere, the campaign against the Jews was not very evident in the many new sights and new things to do in her months in Germany. Now it was coming back to her all too vividly.

"You must realize what would happen to Frau Meix-

59

ner if the Gestapo found out she helped us," the girl was saying urgently. *"A friend of a Jew is a betrayer of his country,"* she quoted.

"I do realize it and I promise I won't tell. Frau Meixner does not even have to know I have been here," Ann said and started to get up, but her movement disturbed Rachel, who gave a slight moan and opened her eyes.

"Go on sleeping, darling," the older girl soothed. "Here, you will be more comfortable." She moved to the edge of the bed and settled the child's head on the pillow.

"She is very quiet," Ann remarked.

"She cannot talk."

"Can't talk!" Ann exclaimed.

"No. She lost her speech the night the Gestapo came to our house."

"Did they do something to her?" Ann asked with horror.

The girl clenched her fists. "They would have to kill *me* first. But she saw Papa being beaten and kicked and she never got over it."

"But *why* were they beating him?" Ann insisted, feeling completely bewildered. "Even when someone is arrested . . ."

"They wanted him to tell them where Mama was hiding. I had better tell you the whole story. Yes, I want to. I feel I can trust you. Do sit down." The girl reached out and pulled Ann onto the bed again. "I have just realized you don't even know my name," she said. "I am Ilse Weiss. Rachel is my sister. I hope I am not talking too fast for you. You know German pretty well, I can see that, and my English is mostly, 'I have the book, but I do not have the pen.'"

"I can follow all right. Please go on," Ann urged.

60

It seemed that the girls' father was a lawyer. Shortly after the Nuremberg Laws appeared, he was forbidden to practice and had to earn his living by doing research work for other lawyers.

"Our mother is a doctor, a children's specialist. She, too, was forbidden to practice, but people from all over Frankfurt used to bring their children to our back door anyway." Ilse's voice was full of pride. "Mama never charged a fee when she saw that people were too poor to afford it. Everyone loved her."

As Ilse talked, Ann could not help noticing how restless she was. Now that she was not holding Rachel, she kept tugging at her sweater, smoothing her hair, or simply drumming her fingers on the blanket. She would have been attractive, if her face had not been so haggard. Pale skin stretched tight across the high cheekbones, dark shadows circled the gray eyes. She breathed rapidly as she went on telling how she had had to transfer to an all-Jewish school; how hard it was to leave her old classmates; how the children next door had once attacked Rachel, thrown mud at her, and called her "Jewish pig."

"But the really bad time for us started about eighteen months ago," Ilse was saying. "One day, my great-uncle was arrested for speeding. It is only a small offense and usually simply means a fine. But because the culprit was a Jew he had to be punished as if he had committed a crime. My great-uncle was sent to prison and his bank account was confiscated."

Ann nodded, remembering Uncle Dick's words: "Jewish people are a good source of income to the government. Whenever a Jewish concern or private capital is confiscated, the money goes to the state."

Ilse took a deep breath. "Papa did all he could to help

my great-uncle," she said. "He still had a few connections in court, but he did not succeed. My great-uncle was sent to a concentration camp."

"Concentration camp?" Ann asked, sure she had misunderstood. "There are concentration camps in Germany? *Now?* But there is no war!"

"Yes, there are camps." Ilse spoke calmly as if she were talking about shops in Kaiser Strasse. "Two very big camps, Osthofen and Westhofen, near the city of Worms. Hundreds of Jews are imprisoned there, and also Germans who have done something that displeased Hitler. But my great-uncle was in another concentration camp, not too far from Frankfurt. Well, when it became clear that nothing could be done to save him, Mama decided she would go personally to the Gestapo and plead with them. Papa told her it would be useless and he tried to stop her, but she still went. At first the guards would not let her in, but she insisted and finally she was admitted to see the man in charge of my great-uncle's case. It turned out that he was a man whose little daughter Mama had saved only a few years ago, when all the other doctors had given up. Although he was a Gestapo man, he had not forgotten what Mama did for his child. My great-uncle was released."

"So he did get free after all!" Ann exclaimed with relief.

Ilse began to drum her fingers again. "Yes, but . . that was not the end of it. Mama never told us his name, but when she was talking with that Gestapo man she realized that he was really against the Nazi regime and that he did not consider it right that innocent people should be sent to concentration camps. I don't know exactly how it came about, but he and Mama made a pact. He would get the release papers and she would drive over to the camp and claim the prisoners. It worked. Between them they saved twenty-seven people in less than one year."

"Wasn't your mother afraid to go to the camp?" Ann asked.

"Mama was never afraid of anything, and Rachel was too young to understand, but Papa and I went through agony every time Mama drove off. It seemed like a miracle every time she came back." Ilse's thin face looked even more haggard as she spoke. Drawing up her knees, she clasped them tight and went on. "Mama never wanted to talk about her trips, except once when she mentioned she had seen the gallows by the camp gate. Oh, yes, she also said that she could not get used to the camp guards' uniform. They wore black with skull and crossbones on the sleeve. 'Death Head Units' they were called. I remember Mama saying, 'It may sound like something from a bad melodrama, but it is real life!' Of course it was not enough just to get people out of the camp. They had to be provided with permits to leave the country, visas, all those things. Mama was becoming more and more involved and Papa was going out of his mind with worry."

"Your mother was *wonderfully* brave," Ann said warmly.

"I know she was," Ilse agreed, "but I was glad when last September Papa announced that he had obtained passports and visas for all of us and that we were leaving Germany for good. The plan was for us to go to Switzerland first, let Mama have a good rest and then settle in England or maybe in America. The main thing of course was to get out of Germany. Switzerland grants entry only to those Jews who have a certain amount of money in a

63

Swiss bank. Luckily, Papa made some investments abroad while he was still practicing law, so there was enough money. We packed fast. Papa made plane reservations. We were to leave on Friday, September the tenth. On Wednesday someone slipped an anonymous letter under our back door. It was not really a letter, just a scribbled note. It said that the Gestapo were going to arrest Mama at any minute. They suspected that one of their members was working against them and wanted Mama to name him. We were terribly frightened and upset, of course, but we were also grateful to whoever had written that note because it gave us time to make plans. It was decided that Mama would go into hiding while Papa, Rachel, and myself would take the plane to Switzerland. Mama left that same day, as soon as it was dark. I was not told where she was going. Papa thought it was safer for me not to know because if I were questioned by the Gestapo I would not have to lie and maybe let something slip out. He assured me that Mama had a very good hiding place and that she would join us abroad very shortly. The next day the Gestapo came . . ."

Ann bent forward, eager not to miss a word. "You mean, to your house?"

"Yes. It was about seven. Rachel and I were going to take Morritz, our dog, for a walk. We were just putting on our coats when Rachel looked through the window and said that two men in long black raincoats were getting out of a car in front of our house. Papa and I looked at each other because the Gestapo dress like that. Someone banged at the front door. Papa pushed us into the pantry and went to open it. It was the Gestapo and they had come to get Mama. When Papa told them he did not know where she was, they would not believe him. At first, they only shouted at him and threatened him, but when he still refused to tell, they threw him on the floor and started to kick him with their boots. The kitchen opens into the anteroom, so we saw it all through the pantry window. As Papa fell, he screamed, 'Run!' I knew he meant us. I wanted to stay with him, but I had to save Rachel. So I grabbed her by the hand and we ran out through the back door. I kept dragging Rachel along and we did not stop until we were several blocks away. It was getting dark and I did not know where to go. The streets looked different and somehow . . . frightening.''

Ilse's eyes stared in front of her, dilated and full of fear, as if she were still standing on that street corner. "I almost turned back home there and then," she said, "because I felt so guilty about leaving Papa. But I also realized that the Gestapo would probably use us to force him to tell them about Mama. The question was what to do next. My parents had many friends in Frankfurt, but we did not need simply a shelter, we needed a hiding place, and who would risk taking us? Then I remembered Frau Meixner. I knew she would be willing. I told Rachel we were going to Mylius Strasse, that it was quite a long way but we did not have any money for a bus or streetcar. That was when I discovered she could not talk any more. I was . . . no, better not to think about that. We walked along and it seemed to me that the trees and houses were falling down around us, but we reached Frau Meixner's home at last and she took us in.''

"But why Frau Meixner?" Ann asked when Ilse paused for breath. "Was she a special friend of your family, or a relative?"

"Didn't I say?" Ilse exclaimed. "Frau Meixner was my nurse. She left to get married when I was three but we always kept in touch. Mama treated Peter whenever he was sick and when Herr Meixner died, Papa took care of all kinds of legal things. I suppose we would have been even closer if Rachel and I were friends with Peter, but he was too young for me and too old for her." She bent her head and murmured desperately, "Yes, Frau Meixner is an angel of kindness! And brave, too, you don't know how brave! But how long are we going to stay here? Papa must be in prison or in a concentration camp and Mama probably thinks we are all safe abroad . . . or maybe she is already abroad herself and looking for us."

"And there is really no way you can get in touch with her?"

Ilse frowned and rubbed her forehead. "She left a telephone number, but we were only to use it in case of extreme emergency. I was supposed to memorize it, but I was so excited and frightened and worried I just could not make it stay in my brain. I told Papa about it and he laughed and said it was the same with him but that he had written the number down in a safe place. Only he never told me where."

Ilse sighed and turning to Rachel moved her into a more comfortable position. Ann slid off the bed. "I think we all need some sleep," she said, then hesitated a little and asked, "Are *you* going to tell Frau Meixner about my barging in on you, or shall I tell her?"

Ilse looked up quickly. "Don't let's say anything to her till after tomorrow. You see, I am planning to slip out again tomorrow night and now—I hope . . . maybe you will be willing to come with me. I need help."

But Ann was not going to make any rash promises. "Help with what?" she asked. "And why shouldn't Frau Meixner know?"

"Because she would never let us go. She would think it too risky. Oh, it is nothing bad. Let me explain. When Papa realized it was the Gestapo at our door, he took the briefcase with all our passports and some valuables in it and threw it on top of the dining room cupboard. It is a very tall cupboard, almost to the ceiling and the top is curved. It is impossible to see the briefcase from below and I am sure the Gestapo never thought of looking up there. I *must* retrieve that briefcase, because of the passports. We each had our own. Papa thought it was safer that way, in case we became separated for some reason. So, maybe Rachel and I could use ours. I don't know when or how, but I do think we will have a better chance if we have those passports, and Papa's too. Mama took hers when she went into hiding."

Ann did not feel sleepy any more. She asked doubtfully, "How do you know you can get into the house? It must be all locked up."

"It is not our own house. There are two floors and we rented the ground one. No one else has come to live there. And I know how to get in. One window does not latch properly, but it is too high for me to reach by myself. I need a leg up."

"But you said it was the ground floor."

"It is. You will understand when you see it. Please say you will come. It may make all the difference to us, and I dare not ask Frau Meixner. She has enough to bear already. Help me, please, help me!"

There was desperate entreaty in the gray eyes. Ann took a deep breath. "What if Rachel wakes again and begins to cry while we're out?"

"So you will do it." For the first time, a smile touched Ilse's pale face. She, too, took a deep breath, but it was a sigh of relief. "I have thought it all out. We will just have to take Rachel with us. It's an awfully long way, but I will see if I can get her to sleep in the afternoon. It will be something for her to be out in the open air."

She reached out and took Ann's hand. "Thank you."

They agreed to start a little after eleven. Frau Meixner and Peter were sure to be asleep by that time.

Feeling so tired she could hardly see where she was going, Ann crept down the stairs to her room. This was something she would not tell Uncle Dick about until they were safely back in England.

8

The Night of October 28th

Frau Meixner and Peter arrived early the next morning. Ann let them in, mumbled something about having had a bad night and retreated to her room. Feeling sleepy and slightly headachy, she stood by the window, watching the overcast sky and the flying snowflakes, and thinking that the two Jewish girls must be cold without proper winter clothes.

"We have only what we had on when we left the house," Ilse had explained. "It was drizzling, so we were wearing our raincoats, and they were our old ones. We always used them when walking Morritz. Frau Meixner bought each of us a change of underwear. She went to the other end of Frankfurt to get it. I am wearing her sweater and she is knitting one for Rachel. I really cannot ask for anything more."

For a while Ann toyed with the idea of offering some of her own clothes to Ilse, then decided against it. Suppose Ilse took offense? Maybe later, when they came to know each other better, she could suggest it.

In the afternoon Ann received a telephone call from Eleonore, who wanted her to come to tea the next day. "About two thirty. I have *loads* to tell you," Eleonore announced. There was a note of mystery in her voice, but Ann paid no attention to it. Night was falling fast and she had more serious things to worry about than Eleonore's secrets.

At last the evening came. Just as Ann had hoped, Frau Meixner and Peter went to bed early. It was ten past eleven when Ann crept up the staircase and scratched at the attic door. Ilse opened it a crack, then backed and motioned Ann to come inside. "I am so glad you've come," she whispered. "I was afraid you might change your mind. Could you wait a few minutes? I am dressing Rachel. We both had to undress and go to bed so that Frau Meixner would not suspect anything."

As Ann waited, she looked around. Now that she was no longer startled and frightened, the attic looked quite different. What she had taken for dirty wallpaper turned out to be pages from old illustrated magazines, yellowed with age: a girl in a lacy dress clasping the neck of a big shaggy dog; two young women in feathered hats smiling from a balcony; hunters with rifles galloping through woods. Behind a partition stood a small table with an electric hot plate on it. On the wall hung a shelf with some dishes.

"Why, it's like a small apartment," Ann said, surprised.

Ilse, who was hurriedly dressing Rachel in every available garment, turned around. "It *is* an apartment," she said. "There is even a shower behind the curtain. When Frau Meixner and her husband first bought the house they had the attic fixed up, hoping to rent it to university students to help with the expenses. Only it did not work out. One of the students was always drunk, another one brought in his friends and they made so much noise the neighbors complained, and several of them left without paying the rent. Finally, the Meixners simply gave up having lodgers and the attic stood empty for years. It was a godsend to us. We can wash ourselves and I warm up the dishes Frau Meixner brings us. Only . . ." her voice trembled, "it is hard to stay locked up day after day, not able even to look through the window."

Rachel was ready at last. She looked a little strange with Frau Meixner's sweater hanging from under her short raincoat.

"Never mind. As long as she is warm, who cares," Ann comforted Ilse who stood looking at her sister and frowning.

But Ilse thought differently. "No, it will never do to attract attention," she declared and began to pin up the sweater.

They tiptoed down the stairs. Ann unlocked the front door. Outside the air was crisp and cold. Bare branches threw black shadows on the white pavement. It had stopped snowing and the wind prevented the fallen snow from drifting. There was only about an inch of it, crunchy and dry underfoot.

For a few seconds, they stood huddled together on the front steps. Then Ann whispered, "Come on! There's no

use creeping along the walls. We would be seen anyway,"
and taking Rachel's hand, she went down the steps.
"Which way?"

"Up to the corner and turn right," Ilse murmured.
Ann glanced at her wristwatch. Quarter to twelve. Not
really very late.

The girls left Mylius Strasse and turned into Grune-
burg Weg. Ann walked easily in her sturdy gumboots,
but the Jewish girls' light shoes kept slipping on the
snow, slowing them down. They met a few people, but no
one paid any attention to them. It was difficult to see
much anyway in the dim light of sparse street lamps.

But as soon as the girls emerged into Eschersheimer
Landstrasse, things changed. It was a wide and busy
street, brilliantly lit, the pavements swept clear of snow
and teeming with people coming from theatres and
movies or going to nightclubs or cabarets. Streetcars
passed, sending blue sparks into the air; a stream of cars
rolled by.

Ann realized that Ilse was right about attracting attention. They had only walked a few steps when heads began
to turn in their direction. "Poor mite. Out at this hour
and in those open shoes," a woman muttered glancing at
Rachel. Two elderly men even stepped back to get a better look at the girls. "There should be a law against children being out alone in the middle of the night," one
said, and the other answered something Ann did not
catch, but it seemed to her she heard the word *"Polizei."*
Tightening her grip on Rachel's hand she hastened on,
afraid to run, but doing her best to get lost in the crowd.

Ilse must have heard too, because she looked frightened and kept pulling up the skimpy collar of her raincoat. "Let's cross here," she whispered. The light

changed. Even with the cars standing still, it took considerable willpower for Ann to pass in front of them. She was trembling when she reached the other side of the street. Rachel weighed heavily on her arm and dragged her feet. "Up Fichardstrasse now," Ilse directed. "Come on, Rachel, you cannot be *that* tired yet."

"She's half asleep," Ann pointed out. "Are we still far from your house?"

Ilse answered nervously, "Not too far if we hurry. This is Bornwiesenweg. The next corner will be Oeder Weg."

It sounded close enough, but Ann was getting tired herself and it seemed hours before Ilse pointed to a street sign with *Oeder Weg* on it.

At last they stopped in front of a gray, two-storied stucco house. Three wide stone steps with wrought-iron railings led to a front door of dark polished wood, topped by a blue and red fanlight. All the windows were dark except one on the second floor. "Who lives up there?" Ann asked in a whisper, her eyes on the light just barely visible behind the curtains.

"Only two elderly ladies. They are Jewish too. Polish Jews. Their name is Zambuski . . . Zambrovski . . . I can't pronounce it. We used to call them the Misses Z. One is a music teacher and the other does fine hand embroidery. Many rich girls give her orders for embroidering their trousseaus."

"Suppose they hear us trying to get in?" Ann asked. "And suppose they take us for burglars and call the police?"

"Oh, they are asleep," Ilse assured her. "It is the night-light that you can see in that window. They always have a night-light. Papa often teased them about it. Come along. This way."

73

Holding Rachel's hand, Ann moved after Ilse, but the child would not go. Making little moaning noises, she kept pulling Ann toward the front door. Her lips moved and Ann thought she could almost read the word *Mutti* on them.

Ilse retraced her steps and, kneeling down, put her arm around the little girl. "We don't live here any more, darling," she whispered, and to Ann, "Let's go before someone sees us and becomes suspicious."

On the left of the house rose the blind wall of a block of apartments. On the right was a garage, separated from the house by a narrow concrete path. "Through here," Ilse whispered.

The passage was dark and the path slippery. Ann walked cautiously, clasping Rachel's hand.

"Watch out!" Ilse warned, and Ann saw a short flight of stone steps. She helped Rachel down and stood looking around in dismay. The backyard was five or six feet below street level. The ground floor windows that seemed so easily accessible from the street, loomed high above the ground. About ten feet, Ann thought grimly, measuring the distance with her eye. She even took a step back to get a better look. "I hate to say it, Ilse," she said at last, "but even if you stand on my back, I don't think you can do it."

"I tried to stand on that," Ilse pointed to a tall garbage can at the other end of the yard, "but the lid was too slippery. If you just give me a push up, I am sure I can manage."

"Well, suppose you do get inside. How are you going to get that briefcase from the top of the cupboard?" Ann asked doubtfully.

"Oh, that is easy. All I have to do is to stand on the

bottom part of the cupboard and reach through all those carvings at the top. I am tall enough for that," Ilse assured her. "Please, let's try."

They tried for a good half hour but without success. Ilse could grasp the windowsill, but she could not pull herself up. They changed places, but Ann's weight was too much for Ilse's narrow shoulders. "I give up," she panted after another try, and jumped to the ground.

"Ha, girls can't climb," someone said, and a short shadow emerged from the alley. As it came nearer, Ann recognized the cap with earmuffs. "Peter!" she exclaimed.

"Peter?" Ilse stepped in front of the boy who was now only a few feet away. "Why did you follow us? What do you want?"

Her tone was unfriendly and Peter answered on the same note. "I heard you two whispering on the landing, so I got up and went after you to make sure you didn't do something stupid and get my mother in trouble."

"It is none of your business," Ilse said hotly. "I am not getting anyone into trouble. All I want is to get something that belongs to us out of the apartment. *You* know we used to live here."

Peter seemed to think it over. "Yes," he said at last, nodding, and suddenly, in a businesslike manner, "What is it that you want to get? I can do it for you."

"Oh, Peter, really?" Ilse was all eagerness. "You think you can climb up there?"

"Of course. That's nothing," Peter boasted.

"Well then, once you get into the apartment . . ." and Ilse began to explain about the briefcase.

Ann suddenly remembered Rachel and anxiously glanced round. The child was standing by the wall, shiv-

75

ering, her small face pinched in the dim light.

"We must go home," she said urgently to Ilse. "Poor Rachel is frozen. Come on. You're only wasting your time. Peter couldn't possibly climb in there."

Peter glared at her. "Can't I? Just watch me!" Taking a flying leap, he caught at the gutter running up one corner of the house and began to climb it.

The girls watched breathlessly. Peter was not quite at the same level as the window, but about a foot to the left of it. Holding on to the gutter, he seemed to inspect the wall.

"Look!" Ilse whispered. Swinging out one foot, Peter grasped the long hook protruding from the wall, swayed sideways and jumped onto the windowsill. "See! I am not holding on to anything!" he announced, standing upright and looking down.

"Never mind, Peter! Get inside!" Ann almost screamed, and Ilse said, lowering her voice, "Thank God that hook held. I hoped it would. Mama used to hang a heavy flowerpot on it."

A slight click came from above. The window opened and Peter vanished inside. He reappeared about five minutes later and threw a dark object at Ilse's feet. The Jewish girl snatched it up joyfully. "It is the briefcase! And the passports are in it. I can feel them."

Ann was not looking at the briefcase. She was watching Peter and hoping he was not going to use the gutter again. Maybe the distance to the ground was not great enough for him to be killed, but he could easily break a leg. Peter interrupted her thoughts with a brisk, *"You,* stand close to the wall. I am going to jump."

Ann was not sure whether he meant her or Ilse, but automatically she moved forward. Before she had time to say a word, Peter caught at the windowsill, his feet dangling in space and neatly dropped onto her shoulders. She staggered, lost her balance and fell, bringing Peter with her.

"Are you all right, Ann? And you, Peter?" Ilse asked anxiously, helping them to get up.

"No harm done," Ann answered, brushing the snow off her coat. "What about you, Peter?"

He shrugged his shoulders, "I'm all right, but something funny is going on up there." He jerked his thumb in the direction of the second floor windows.

"What do you mean?" both girls asked simultaneously.

"I needed something to knock that briefcase off the top of the cupboard," Peter explained. "It was too high for me to reach. All your things are still in the apartment. I found a broom and knocked the thing down with the handle. When I went into the front room I heard voices coming from above. There was a woman crying and a man shouting."

Ilse twisted her hands nervously. "I can't hear anything."

"I told you it came from the front of the house." Peter's voice was tense and impatient. "Let's get out of here."

Ilse took Rachel's hand. "All right. We are ready. Coming, Ann?"

Peter stopped them. "Wait! Do we have to go back down that alley by the garage? What's behind there?" He pointed at the brick wall that enclosed the yard.

"Just another backyard," Ilse told him. "The people who live there have two vicious dogs, but they are usually locked up for the night. We *could* go that way."

It was Rachel who settled the matter. She suddenly

plumped down on the ground and began to cry. "Rachel, sweetheart . . ." Ilse began, but Ann cut her short. "She is frozen and tired. We can't make her climb walls. Let's just slip out quietly."

Ilse did not argue. Her own lips were blue with cold and she was obviously making an effort not to let her teeth chatter. Peter leading, they went up the steps and into the passage.

It struck Ann that there was more light now than before. They had almost reached the street when she saw the reason. A van with headlights blazing was standing in front of the house. Two men in long black raincoats and military boots were hustling two elderly women down the steps. A third man, in the same uniform, was waiting by the van.

The four children cowered in the passage, afraid to move. Ann thought she could never forget the expression of bewilderment, fright, and utter helplessness stamped on the faces of the old ladies. Both were dressed in old-fashioned clothes that seemed to have been flung on in a hurry. Black bonnets were set askew on their straggling gray hair. The one who looked slightly the younger was carrying a bundle made of a pillowcase in one hand, while adjusting her spectacles with the other. The other woman looked older and more frail. She walked with shuffling steps and kept asking piteously, "But what have we done, Sister? What have we done?"

"*Schweigen!*" the man shouted menacingly and the woman shrank back, drawing her shawl tighter around her shoulders.

Standing in the shadows of the passage, the girls and Peter pressed close to each other. Ilse whispered, "Those are Gestapo men and they are arresting the Misses Z. But why?" Peter kept silent. Ann noticed that he had pulled his woolen cap almost to his eyebrows.

"*Schneller! Schneller!*" the men shouted, pushing the women toward the van. The younger one gave a slight scream, "My glasses!" and dropping on her knees, she began to grope about in the snow. "I meant to have them repaired. I can't see without them."

A heavy boot shot out. There was a crunch of breaking glass and a trembling voice exclaimed, "Oh, no! What am I going to do now? Sister! Where . . ."

Loud barking drowned her last words. A small dog, all long red fur and bushy tail, his ears standing upright, ran out of the house and made for the man who was holding the younger woman by the elbow and forcing her into the van.

"Morritz!" Ilse gasped. The dog snarled and its jaws closed around the man's leg. Swearing, he let the woman go and whipping a gun out of his pocket fired straight at the dog's head. But the bullet only ricocheted against the stone steps, missing the animal. "*Donnerwetter!*" the man grumbled and raised the gun again.

Ann felt something brush past her. She made a grab at Rachel, but it was too late. With a strange, inarticulate wail, the child ran toward the dog, waving her hands and slithering on the trodden-down snow. Forgetting all precaution, Ann raced after her, screaming at the top of her voice, "Don't shoot!"

At that same moment another shot rang out. This time the man must have taken a better aim for there was a yelp and Ann saw a trail of blood on the snow as the animal ran barking in Rachel's direction. The little girl sank on the snow and the dog jumped into her arms.

"Rachel! Is she hurt?" Ilse panted, running up. She

79

was bending over the child when a pale face appeared in the door of the van and they heard the quavering voice of the older woman. "Sister, there is Ilse Weiss! And little Rachel too! Oh God! They have shot her."

The Gestapo man, the gun still in his hand, muttered something to his companions and strode toward the girls who were trying to pull Rachel to her feet. *"Halt!"* he ordered. But Ann was already dragging Rachel away. Peter was nowhere to be seen. Only Ilse remained, standing still as if mesmerized by the order.

Suddenly, a shrill whistle came from the depths of the passage. Ann recognized the sound. Peter always whistled like that when coming home from school. The whistle broke the spell. Ilse swung around and ran. She caught Rachel's other arm and she and Ann half carried, half dragged the little girl along, the dog hard at their heels.

The man shouted *"Halt!"* again, but the girls did not stop. If he decides to shoot, he can't possibly miss us, Ann thought. No shot came, but the heavy breathing and pounding of boots sounded terribly close. Rachel seemed to get heavier every minute. Ann's arm felt as if it were being wrenched from its socket, her chest hurt, something pricked in her left side. Where was Peter?

Ilse gasped something that sounded like, "Over there," and Ann saw a red mitten waving frantically from behind a lamppost. Setting her teeth, she made a dash forward, just as the Gestapo man slipped on the frozen edge of the pavement and crashed down on his hands and knees.

This gave them time. They rounded a corner, almost knocking Peter down. A few steps away there was an open gate. "In here," Peter hissed. They all ran through the gate—even Rachel was moving now—through someone's backyard and through into another alley.

"I must rest a second," Ann panted. Letting go of Rachel's hand she leant against the wall. Ilse, who looked deadly pale, stopped too, and thrust her hand down the front of her coat. "I have not lost it!" she announced triumphantly, showing a corner of the briefcase. "I threw it inside here while we were still in that alley."

"Never mind that thing," Peter interrupted her roughly. "What about the dog? He is bleeding."

Ilse stooped over the dog who was licking Rachel's face. "It is only a scratch," she said. "Right at the top of his ear. The bullet only grazed it. The Misses Z. must have sheltered him when we left."

"Well, he can live with us now," Peter declared. "I can take him for walks and feed him. We . . . Look!"

A police van flashed by at the end of the street and disappeared into the darkness.

"Was it the same one?" Ilse asked, her chin trembling.

Peter shook his head, frowning. "I don't think so. The other one was smaller. Let's go home. It isn't very safe here for you, and I'm starving!"

Starving! Ann felt nothing but an overwhelming desire to crawl into bed and sleep and sleep and not remember anything.

They walked on slowly, Rachel stumbling at every step. It was Peter's idea to take a different route home and he was right because this way they avoided the part of Eschersheimer Landstrasse where they would again attract attention. Only it took them over two hours to get home.

It was almost four o'clock in the morning when they turned into Mylius Strasse, Rachel in Ann's arms. The kitchen windows were lighted. Frau Meixner must have discovered that they were gone. . . .

81

9

Explanations

There are mornings when it would be better not to get up, Ann thought grimly, sitting up in bed. She hoped that by now Frau Meixner would have calmed down a little.

She had been hysterical when the girls and Peter, followed closely by Morritz, filed in through the front door. From a torrent of words intermingled with sobs, they gathered that she had awakened a little after midnight and had gone downstairs for a drink of water. As she passed Ann's door, she noticed that it was not quite shut, and, looking in, found the bed empty. She then checked Peter's room, and then the attic. All the children were gone ! Panic stricken, she could not think what to do. She could scarcely call the police, and she did not dare to disturb Doctor Fromm at such an hour. She had spent the time pacing from room to room in a state of mounting terror, peering through each window in turn, hoping to see them returning.

At this point Ilse had suddenly swayed and crumpled to the floor in a dead faint, and by the time Frau Meixner had finished fussing around with hot water bottles and warm milk she was too exhausted to go on with her tirade. Declaring that Ilse and Rachel could not sleep in the attic that night because they needed to be looked after, she put them both into her own double bed. She would spend what was left of the night on the sofa.

But the lull did not last long. As soon as Frau Meixner heard the details of the night's events from Peter and Ann, she became hysterical all over again. The Gestapo was probably coming at any minute! They were all going to perish in a concentration camp! She was sure the house was already surrounded!

It was almost dawn before Ann reached her room. Glancing through the window, she saw Peter armed with a big broom. He was carefully obliterating their footsteps in the snow.

She was sure she would sleep like a log until at least noon, but instead she kept tossing and turning and when she finally dozed off she was disturbed by muffled sounds. The telephone rang . . . then the doorbell . . . there were steps . . . voices. . . . Now she was fully awake and might as well get up.

When she came downstairs, she found Doctor Fromm drinking coffee at the kitchen table and talking to Frau Meixner. Morritz lay by the stove nibbling at a piece of roll.

"Oh, Fraulein Anna, you should not be up so early,"

Frau Meixner exclaimed, and the doctor said, "I am afraid I woke you with my telephone call. I had to go out on night duty and noticed the lights on in Frau Meixner's house. Naturally I was worried. Now that you know our secret—" he forced a tired smile—"you will understand why I was anxious. I had to find out if anything was wrong."

"Everything is wrong!" exclaimed Frau Meixner. "That dog now," she pointed at Morritz. "He will lead the Gestapo straight to us! Imagine—Peter wanted to take him out this morning! *Nein, nein und nein,* I told him. Everybody in the street knows we have no dog; he would be noticed at once. I have put some newspapers on the cellar floor. He must go down there when he needs to."

"Do you think the Gestapo might really come here?" Ann asked the doctor when Frau Meixner went upstairs to see if Ilse and Rachel were awake.

The doctor finished his coffee before answering. He put the cup down carefully. "I think it is possible, even probable. From what Frau Meixner has told me, I gather you got away safely last night. That was fortunate, more fortunate than you can imagine. But they have ways and means of finding people. They may have already contacted the blockfuhrers to find out if anyone of them has noticed something peculiar in his block—and our blockfuhrer, unfortunately, is intelligent and observant."

"Blockfuhrer?" Ann asked.

"Every block of houses has a blockfuhrer," the doctor explained. "He is supposed to keep an eye on people and inform the authorities about anything suspicious or out of the ordinary. You have undoubtedly met our blockfuhrer in the street. He lives only a few doors away."

84

"Yes, I think I know him," Ann said pensively. "Is he short, with a square face? I saw him only a few days ago, standing by the lamppost just opposite our front door. Sometimes he just walks up and down the pavement. I remember him because his pipe smells so awful."

The doctor nodded. "That's the one. He smokes some vile cheap tobacco. And if you saw him several times, it probably means he is watching this house in particular, though that may well be because of *you*."

"I suppose it might be," Ann whispered, a sudden chill running down her spine.

Doctor Fromm took off his glasses, rubbed them with his handkerchief, and put them on again. He glanced at his old-fashioned gold pocket watch. "See now, *liebchen*," he said, stroking his chin, "this is what we are going to do. You must go to the hospital at once and see your uncle. Tell him all about last night. He may . . . er . . . he must be told. In the meantime, Frau Meixner and I will be busy. The important thing, of course, is to prevent the Gestapo from finding those poor children, and with God's help it can be done."

"Are you going to hide them in your house?" Ann asked doubtfully.

The doctor shook his head. "No, Minna could never keep it secret. That is why she is not allowed to come here any longer. She used to have the run of the house, but Frau Meixner was afraid she might go up to the attic. No, we have something else in mind." He lowered his voice. "When the attic was remodeled, storage space was left between the northern wall and the new partition. However, it was so narrow that no trunk would fit it, so Frau Meixner never used it. Later, when she was papering the little apartment with those magazine cuttings, she covered the door leading to the storage space because she thought it made the room look neater. Luckily she still has those old magazines. The girls will hide in the space and we will paper over the door again when they are safely inside."

"How long will they have to stay in there?" Ann asked, horrified. "And what about Morritz?"

Doctor Fromm made a helpless gesture. "We can only hope it will not be for long. A few hours if we are lucky— the time it takes the Gestapo to search the house, assuming they come and come soon. But it is best to be prepared. About the dog, we shall see. Now, off with you. It is too early for visiting hours, but I can give you a pass."

As Ann was carrying her plate and cup to the sink, the soft music floating from Frau Meixner's small radio stopped and the announcer said, "We repeat the previous bulletin. The mass deportation of Polish Jews which was started last night is still in progress. So far, over three hundred Jews of Polish origin have been deported from Frankfurt."

"So that's why we saw all those police vans!" exclaimed Ann. "But Ilse and Peter said it wasn't the police, it was the Gestapo who arrested the poor old ladies."

The doctor did not seem disposed to let Ann linger and discuss the matter. "Yes, yes," he said impatiently. "I heard the bulletin earlier and wondered about that. I think it can only mean the Gestapo is still hoping to discover something about Doctor Weiss's whereabouts from those poor women. I am afraid they are in for severe interrogation. Now hurry, child. It is late."

"It's not even nine yet," Ann objected. "Maybe I should go later, in ordinary visiting hours, and stay now to help you and Frau Meixner with the attic."

86

"No! You are to go *now*." The doctor was very emphatic. "Frau Meixner and I can manage quite well. There is no need for you to stay."

A little surprised at the doctor's insistence, Ann obediently went to get her coat. She was just closing the front door behind her when a slightly built woman wrapped in a brown shawl came up, asked breathlessly, *"Frau Meixner zu Hause?"* and without waiting for Ann's answer pushed past her into the house. Ann wondered who she could be and was tempted to turn back, but Doctor Fromm's instructions had been very firm. She sighed, and set off for the streetcar.

The sky was still overcast, but it was milder now and the streets were covered with slush instead of snow. The streetcar was not crowded. It was Saturday and many offices and shops were closed.

Ann found Uncle Dick in the best of spirits, surrounded by the morning papers. "Welcome!" he cried cheerfully. "What a gratifyingly early visit! I was not sure whether to expect you at all today, considering all your social obligations."

But his smile vanished when Ann said soberly, "Uncle Dick, I must tell you something."

"What's wrong?" he asked quickly. "Sit down."

Pulling her chair close to the bed, Ann bent forward and blurted out, "Frau Meixner is hiding two Jewish girls in her house and the Gestapo is after them."

She was startled by Uncle Dick's reaction. "For heaven's sake," he snapped, "shut up, and close the door!"

She did so and came back to her chair, but before she had time to start again, the door opened wide and an elderly nurse, crackling with starch, appeared on the threshold. "Herr Lindsay, you know you need fresh air.

These rooms become too hot—" she began, but Uncle Dick shouted, "To blazes with your fresh air! Can't I have a private talk with my niece?" There was a gulp, more crackling of the starched uniform and the door closed noiselessly but firmly.

"Now," Uncle Dick ordered. "Tell me everything. But keep your voice down."

He listened attentively, without interrupting, and when Ann finished with an anxious, "Do you think the Gestapo will really come to Frau Meixner's house?" he said, "I'm afraid they will." He pondered for a moment, tapping the stem of his pipe on the edge of the bed table. "Let me ask you a few questions," he said at last. "You say that the little girl ran to her dog and that you ran after her, screaming at the man not to shoot. Were you screaming in German or English? Think carefully. It's important."

Ann screwed up her eyes and bit her lower lip. It had happened so fast and she had been so frightened, it was hard to remember.

"Well?" Her uncle sounded impatient.

Ann opened her eyes. "German."

"Are you sure? Quite sure?"

"Yes. I remember I was surprised myself that I knew how to say 'shoot' in German. Why? Would it have mattered if I had yelled in English?"

"Yes, because you could be traced much more easily. Next question: What were you wearing?"

"My old coat. The one you said was so hideous."

"Good! It's totally nondescript. One more thing: Did the Gestapo men have much of a chance to see your face?"

Ann considered this. "No-o. Not really. I had my

woolen scarf on and I'd pulled it forward because my ears were cold."

"Well, we'll hope for the best. Now listen. If the Gestapo come to the house, pretend you can understand German but not speak it. Just say '*Ya*' and '*Nein*.'"

"All right, if you think I'd better. But, Uncle Dick," Ann's voice rose in a wail of distress, "you keep talking about *me*. What about Ilse and Rachel? What's going to happen to *them*?"

Uncle Dick frowned. "Ann my dear, how can I say, sitting in this hospital room? I only wish I could help! I'll be frank with you: things look bad to me. You say that the girls and their father all have passports and visas. So far the Germans are not trying to detain Jews. They *want* them to leave Germany. If the girls' father is still being held, it can only mean that the Gestapo is trying to get through him to his wife. The same applies to the girls, but even more so, I'm afraid. If Doctor Weiss hears that her daughters are in the Gestapo's hands, she may well surrender herself. You do understand all this, I hope."

"Yes, Uncle Dick. I see what you mean." Ann rose and picked up her coat. "And I think I'd better go back now." She waited for her uncle to say something but as he remained silent, she asked anxiously, "Why don't you say something? Uncle Dick, are you all right?"

He moved impatiently, winced with pain and thrust a pillow deeper behind his back. "Of course I'm all right. I was only thinking. . . . Perhaps the best thing would be to send you back to England right now. The nurse could make a plane reservation and your luggage could be sent over later. There's no need for you to go back at all to Mylius Strasse."

Ann looked at him aghast. So this was the reason Doctor Fromm had insisted she should see her uncle! "I can't leave!" she exclaimed. "Uncle Dick, *please* don't make me go. Leave Ilse and Rachel and Frau Meixner as if I didn't care what happened to them? Maybe I could help them! I *want* to help."

"Getting in the Gestapo's way is not a game," he reminded her drily. "If that blockfuhrer has reported something out of the ordinary going on in Frau Meixner's house—on top of her taking in an English girl, which will certainly have been reported—it won't take long to establish her connection with the Weiss family. There is her record of employment, for instance. Don't forget you're involved in something Hitler's government considers a crime."

"I know, and I *am* scared, but I want to stay. Anyhow," Ann added defiantly, "you can't sent me home because my home is with you."

Uncle Dick eyed her keenly, then said with a wry smile, "If that's the way you feel, you might as well stay. It's possible you could be useful as camouflage. So remember what I told you: be very English. And wait a moment; don't leave yet. Have you got a comb with you?"

Ann stared. "A comb?"

"Yes. Remember I gave you a case with a pocket comb to carry in your handbag?"

"Oh yes . . . it's here somewhere." Ann searched her bag, thinking she could hardly confess to Uncle Dick that she had used the comb to groom Morritz that very morning.

"Never mind. Use mine. It's in that drawer. Got it? Good. Now comb your hair straight back. That's it. You look at least a couple of years younger than you really are. How do you like it?"

"I don't like it at all," Ann muttered, looking into the mirror above the washstand, but there was no denying that it made her look much more childish.

Uncle Dick was unsympathetic. "Too bad. Just wear it that way until the danger is over. Perhaps Frau Meixner can lend you a hair-ribbon. We'll hope the Gestapo description is of an 'older girl.' "

"Eleonore will think I look funny when she sees me this afternoon," Ann commented, still examining herself in the mirror.

Uncle Dick's crooked eyebrows met. "You're going to visit that girl today? That's a complication! But perhaps it's for the best. Only, be very careful when you talk to her, won't you? She may repeat something you say to her father, and the nurses tell me he is an important figure in the Nazi party here."

Ann was on the point of telling Uncle Dick that it was not Eleonore's father but Eleonore herself who was the danger, but decided against it. No use alarming him further—he might really carry out his threat to send her home. She wanted to get back to Mylius Strasse as soon as possible.

"No, I'll be very careful," she said, and went out leaving the door carefully open behind her for the benefit of the white-starched nurse.

10

Behind the Partition

All the way home, Ann became more and more anxious. Sitting in the streetcar, she counted every stop and glanced nervously at every street sign. When the familiar stop came in sight at last she jumped out so hurriedly that she stubbed her toe against the edge of the pavement.

She relaxed a little as she approached the house. Everything looked as usual. There was a car parked near Number 16, but not directly in front of it. Reassured, she unlocked the front door and walked in. She had barely gone two steps when two men came out of the kitchen. One was elderly, with a balding head and small sharp eyes. The other was very tall with a thin face and a small scar under the left eye. Ann recognized him immediately. It was the man who had shot at Morritz and chased her and the others in Oeder Weg.

At Ann's entrance, the older man fixed his eyes on her and rapped out, "Do you live here?"

Ann nodded. Her throat felt too tight for speaking and besides, Uncle Dick had told her to pretend she could not speak German. The man gave her another piercing glance and called, "Gunter!"

The younger man, who was marking something in a notebook, came closer. Behind him appeared Frau Meixner's blanched face. The older man pointed at Ann. *"Gunter, ist das das Madchen?"*

Ann froze. Gunter's eyes traveled slowly from her hair to her face, down her coat and even to her feet. Hardly daring to breathe, Ann waited, wondering why the blue runner on the hall floor suddenly seemed a mile long.

"Nein . . ." Gunter drawled at last. "She was older."

Ann thought the other man answered, "Are you sure?" and then Frau Meixner began to explain that Ann was her lodger and a British subject. Ann was not really listening. All she wanted was to sit down because her knees felt so wobbly. Automatically, she headed for the nearest chair which happened to be by the door. Gunter apparently interpreted her movement as an attempt to get out of the house because he barked, *"Halt! Hier bleiben,"* and the older man translated in broken English, "You no go out."

Ann sat down and leaned her head against the wall, wishing her heart would stop jumping up and down. She felt Gunter's eyes on her, probing, watching. Maybe he was not as sure as he pretended to be? She was almost glad when he disappeared down the basement steps, then remembered Morritz. Was the dog downstairs? No, probably not, because Gunter was already coming back. His

93

curt, "Nothing there," made Ann breathe again. She rather hoped the kitchen and the parlor would be searched next, but the men were already mounting the stairs. Ann caught the word "attic" and her heart turned over. She got up and followed them. Frau Meixner walked in front of her, heaving herself from step to step as if she had weights attached to her feet.

They were about halfway up, when Ann heard steps behind her. She turned around. It was Peter. He was probably just back from one of his meetings, because he was in his Hitler's Youth uniform. Not that Ann had much thought to spare for Peter. The latch clicked. The attic door opened. Ann strained her ears. Suppose Rachel gave one of her strange little moans, or Morritz growled. He must be with the girls since he was not in the basement. Or maybe no one was in the attic. The doctor and Frau Meixner could have made different arrangements.

Tense as she was, Ann could not help noticing the way the two Gestapo men entered the attic. They did it in one long, stealthy step, moving sideways, with their hands on the gun pockets which now bulged visibly under their black raincoats.

Ann thought fleetingly: What a lot of bother for a fourteen-year-old girl and a baby, then forgot all about it in her panic fear of what was going to happen next. Forcing herself to mount one more step, she looked over Frau Meixner's shoulder.

In the light of the watery November sun, the attic looked peaceful, neat, and clean. Almost too clean. The floor was scrubbed, the windows gleamed, the sparse furniture was free of dust. This looks too *lived in,* Ann thought. It needs a few cobwebs, a few old trunks here and there.

94

The Gestapo men looked around, their faces impassive. The older man said, "This is an apartment. Who lives here?"

Frau Meixner, to whom the question was addressed, opened her mouth and spoke as if she could not get enough breath. "I used to let it, but . . . I have no lodgers now. I am planning to let it again."

Gunter opened his notebook and checked something. "Correct," he reported to the other man who was obviously his superior.

What was correct? Ann wondered. That Frau Meixner used to rent the attic? Maybe the Gestapo men would leave now that they had checked on it.

But they were not going away. Instead, they began a thorough search of the room—peering under the mattress, squeezing the pillows, shaking the small china cupboard built into the wall, going into the tiny bathroom. . . .

From Frau Meixner's terrified look, Ann realized that the girls must be hidden behind the partition as planned. When Gunter began to tap the walls, she looked as if she were going to scream. Ann felt sick as she watched Gunter come nearer and nearer to the northern wall, his long fingers feeling over every inch of the magazine pages. Sometimes he scratched the paper with his nails, and for one sickening moment, he laid his ear against the wall.

Ann bit her lower lip and stood rigid. Gunter turned toward the older man and said something she did not understand. He had a heavy Bavarian accent which made his speech difficult to follow. Whatever he said, his superior only grunted. "These have been here since the house was built," he said disdainfully, eyeing the yellowed illustrations.

95

Gunter suddenly bent forward and pounced on something on the floor behind the bed. As he straightened up, Ann saw that he was holding the old clown Rachel used to play with. Without a word, he turned and showed the toy to Frau Meixner. There was triumph on his face.

"Das ist mein!" Peter stepped forward and held out his hand. Gunter's jaw dropped. With an ironical, "At your age!" he flung the clown at Peter.

Something wet trickled down Ann's chin. She touched it with her finger and realized that she had bitten her lip so hard it was bleeding. She put her hand to her mouth to hide the blood and stood watching the Gestapo men leave the attic. At the door, the older man turned round. "No one is to stay behind. Come out of here," he ordered.

The search went on. Every inch of the house was inspected, from the wardrobes in the bedrooms to the drawers of the kitchen cupboard. The men even made another rapid inspection of the attic. Peter followed them everywhere, a half-admiring, half-fearful expression on his freckled face.

Ann and Frau Meixner were ordered to sit in the parlor. Frau Meixner was softly sobbing into her apron; Ann pressed her handkerchief to her already swelling lip and kept her eyes on her wristwatch. The search had been going on for more than four hours.

At quarter to three the telephone rang. Gunter answered it and silently handed the receiver to Ann. It was Eleonore and she wanted to know why Ann was so late. She spoke in English and Ann answered in the same language, simply saying that something unexpected had happened. Then she heard the maid's voice saying something and Eleonore suddenly ended her call with a rapid, "I understand. Tomorrow then, at the same time," and rang off.

Gunter stood by listening attentively to everything that was said. "Colonel Von Waldenfels's daughter?" he asked when Ann had finished. There was respect in his voice. The older man seemed impressed too. Ann could see that the mention of the colonel's name made them much less suspicious. After that they made only a superficial search of the parlor, and left. The car spluttered outside, the tires swished, and they were gone. Ten minutes later, Doctor Fromm arrived through the back door. "Not yet," he told Frau Meixner who was already rushing up the stairs. "We must wait for an hour or so. The Gestapo has been known to return unexpectedly. We must take no chances."

"We will find their frozen bodies! It is ice cold in that hole!" Frau Meixner shouted hysterically, but Doctor Fromm only answered, "They are well wrapped up and remember, we are doing it for their own sake."

Ann knew she ought to try to calm Frau Meixner, but instead she began to cry herself. Something inside her suddenly snapped. With her head on the kitchen table, she sobbed and between sobs, she poured out how Uncle Dick had wanted to send her back to England, how terrible it had been when Gunter inspected the walls, how she had been expected at Eleonore's house and could not go. At this point, she broke down completely, repeating over and over again that she could not go to Eleonore's. It sounded as if she was crying merely because she had missed a tea party, and this made her cry even more.

Frau Meixner ran to get a glass of water. Doctor Fromm held it to Ann's lips and told her to take little

97

sips. At first he stroked her hair and kept saying, "Calm down, liebchen. You are just tired," but when she went on crying, he abruptly changed his tone and said, "Look here. It is more than an hour since the Gestapo left. It is unlikely they will come back now. Pull yourself together. We need your help with the girls."

Ann gulped and put the glass down. To her surprise, her knees felt quite steady as she followed the doctor up the attic steps. Behind them came Frau Meixner, sighing and muttering to herself. Hobnailed shoes clattered across the kitchen. Peter was coming up too.

Doctor Fromm knocked on the partition. "They are gone, Ilse!" he called softly. "We will have you out in a minute."

Ilse's voice called something in answer. Ann began to tear at the yellowed magazine pages. Frau Meixner and the others helped her. Soon a narrow door appeared. The doctor opened it and vanished inside, with Peter after him.

"Ach Himmel!" Frau Meixner exclaimed as Doctor Fromm came out carrying Rachel. The child's head was propped against his shoulder. Her eyes were closed and she was breathing heavily. Peter followed, Morritz's limp form in his arms.

"They are not dead," the doctor said quickly seeing Ann's frightened stare. "I had to give them both a sedative to keep them quiet. Even a slight sound would have attracted attention." He raised his voice, "Peter, leave the dog alone. Don't try to wake him up. It is bad for him. He will come round by himself."

Peter, who was kneeling over Morritz, looked up scowling. "I am *not* trying to wake him up. I am only *looking* at him and I think it is a rotten shame to make him half-dead like this. He is a *good* dog. If he were mine, he would be romping in the garden and we could run races. But he belongs to dirty Jews and . . ."

"Schweigen! Schweigen!" Frau Meixner flew at her son with her hand raised menacingly. "It is that Hitler's Youth! *They* make you so wicked."

Doctor Fromm touched her shoulder. "Frau Meixner, *bitte!* Peter does not mean it really. Would you please take Rachel from me. My rheumatic arm can't take the weight much longer. And you, liebchen," he turned to Ann. "Please see to Ilse. I thought she was behind me."

But Ilse was just emerging from behind the partition. She was pale, with enormous dark circles under her eyes, and as she stepped into the room she took a deep breath, then pressed her hands under her breastbone. "There was so little air," she murmured. "I dozed off once. Then I woke up. I heard voices. I realized the Gestapo *had* come. I could hear their steps . . . coming closer . . . closer. Someone began to touch the wall . . . right by my head. I thought he would hear us breathing. I put my hand over Rachel's mouth. I could have killed her. If I ever hear that rustle of paper again . . ." She did not finish. Bending over, she vomited on the attic floor.

Doctor Fromm looked at Rachel, who was beginning to moan and struggle in Frau Meixner's arms. "Let's take them both downstairs," he suggested. "They must be made comfortable."

Frau Meixner's faded blue eyes blinked. "But, Doctor, the Gestapo . . ."

"They can find them here as easily as downstairs," Doctor Fromm answered grimly, and taking Ilse's arm he

99

drew her gently toward the stairs. "Come, my dear, you will feel better after a rest."

Ann spent the next hour filling hot water bottles, warming milk, and getting out extra blankets. Rachel drank some milk and was soon peacefully asleep in Frau Meixner's large comfortable bed, but Ilse kept tossing and repeating. "They were so close . . . so close . . ." At last her voice sank to a whisper and her head dropped onto the pillow.

"She will sleep now," the doctor said. "I have given her an injection."

Frau Meixner installed herself in an armchair by the bed. "I will stay with the girls for a while," she declared.

"Shall I bring you a cup of coffee?" Ann offered.

"An excellent idea!" Doctor Fromm nodded approvingly. "And then you and I and Peter will have some coffee too and maybe a bite to eat."

When they came into the kitchen, they found Peter squatting on the floor, feeding Morritz from a salad bowl.

"Your mother won't like your using that bowl," Ann warned.

Peter glared at her. "I don't care. Everyone was fussing about those two silly girls upstairs and nobody paid any attention to *him*. He tried to walk, but he kept bumping into the furniture. So I took him into the yard and it did him good."

The doctor said wearily, "You should not have done that. It is dangerous."

Peter shrugged his shoulders. "So what?"

Morritz finished his bread and milk, licked his chops and streaked up the stairs. Peter looked after him, muttering resentfully, "What does he go to *her* for?" Then he scrambled up and stalked out through the back door.

"It is dark outside," Ann exclaimed. "And he has only his sweater on."

"Leave him alone," Doctor Fromm advised. "It is a difficult situation for him. He does not quite know how to handle it. A short walk won't do him any harm."

Ann took some coffee and a sandwich up to Frau Meixner, then she and the doctor installed themselves at the kitchen table, eating, and talking in low voices.

Doctor Fromm drained his cup and smiled at Ann. "Thank you for the supper, liebchen. It is certainly a comfort to have you here. But of course your uncle is right to want to send you back to England."

Ann instantly became alarmed. "Oh, Doctor! Please don't tell Uncle Dick to send me away. I don't want to go until it is all over."

Doctor Fromm leaned back in his chair. He looked tired and old again. *"Until it is all over,* you say, easily. But the question is: Just *how* is it going to be over? When Frau Meixner first took the girls in, she was sure their father would be released very soon and then they would all be able to leave the country. But it did not happen that way. Ilse, alone, would be easier to hide. But the child . . . and now the dog! How long will our luck hold? The Gestapo worked fast. If the blockfuhrer's wife had not warned Frau Meixner they were coming, we might not have been ready in time."

"The blockfuhrer's wife!" Ann gasped. "Was that the woman I met when I was leaving the house to go to the hospital?"

The doctor nodded. "Yes. She is an old friend of Frau Meixner. They went to school together. Ah, here is Frau Meixner herself!"

Ann turned and saw Frau Meixner, cup in hand, coming down the stairs. "I only wanted some more coffee," she explained. "The girls are sleeping peacefully. *Himmel!* What is that?"

There was a crash, accompanied by the tinkling of broken glass. It seemed to Ann that the whole kitchen shook.

Frau Meixner screamed, Doctor Fromm swore. Ann saw a gaping hole in one of the glass panels of the back door. A large brick lay on the floor surrounded by splinters of glass.

"Peter!" the doctor roared.

The door opened, scattering the remains of the glass, and Peter slid in. "I did it," he announced defiantly.

The doctor fixed him with a stern eye. "I know you did. But why?"

"Because I had to." Peter's voice was hard and at the same time choked with tears. "I stood outside and I thought . . . I thought if I had only told the Gestapo about those Jewish girls, I would have earned a citation in front of the whole Hitler's Youth! I would have been a hero, and . . . and I would have kept the dog. Instead I had to pretend that stupid clown was mine as if I were five years old. I just had to do something! And I did it! And I don't care!"

Frau Meixner opened her mouth to say something, but Doctor Fromm stopped her with a firm, "Please leave it to me." Addressing Peter again, he said, "Go upstairs and get into bed. You will feel better tomorrow. And take a biscuit for the dog with you."

Peter looked at his mother, then at the doctor again, and vanished silently.

Frau Meixner produced an old kitchen towel and began to stuff the hole. Ann helped to sweep up the broken glass and started to wash up, but the doctor insisted that she, too, must go to bed. "You are tired out, child," he said. "It has been a difficult day for us all."

Frau Meixner sat down suddenly at the table, her face in her hands. Making a hasty sign for Ann to leave the room, Doctor Fromm pulled up a chair close to her. "You must understand how the boy feels . . ." Ann heard him say as she slowly mounted the stairs. The doctor was right: she was so weary she could barely put one foot before the other. But over and beyond her weariness, she was sick with fear.

11

Talking to Minna

"Your Herr Uncle was surprised to hear you had gone
to bed," Frau Meixner told Ann next morning. Uncle
Dick had called later that evening but Ann was asleep. "I
told him we had all had a very hard day and he seemed to
understand."

"I'll call him after breakfast and tell him everything,"
Ann said eagerly. But Uncle Dick stopped her after the
very first word. "Tell me the whole story when you come
here," he said quickly. "I suppose you had to postpone
your tea party? Going this afternoon? Well, enjoy yourself."

Ann felt a little guilty about going to Eleonore's, for it
meant leaving Frau Meixner alone to look after Ilse and
Rachel. The little girl was happily playing with Morritz

and did not need any special care, but Ilse was feverish and restless. Whenever she dropped off to sleep, she woke up crying and asking Frau Meixner to save her and Rachel from the Gestapo. Ann brought her lunch on a tray, arranged as temptingly as possible, but Ilse could not keep anything down.

"Nerves," Doctor Fromm diagnosed. "It is hardly surprising after all she has been through. Let her rest and try to give her clear broth or tea with lemon. You, child, must go out and forget everything, or we will have you sick too."

Rather reluctantly, Ann went, but she did feel better as soon as she was out of doors. The weather was bright and frosty; a Sunday peace reigned over Frankfurt. People in the street looked as if they were merely strolling for the pleasure of breathing the invigorating air. A group of children passed Ann, obviously on their way to a birthday party for they had presents in their hands. Ann thought how nice it would have been if Ilse and Rachel were with her. She and Ilse would walk together and Rachel would run in front of them with Morritz on a lead. A deep anger suddenly welled up in her heart. Such simple pleasures as taking a walk and enjoying the sun and air! Yet the two girls were denied even these just because they were Jewish. Clenching her hands in the pockets of her coat, she turned the corner sharply and almost bumped into a nun, who murmured something and stepped back.

"I am so sorry," Ann apologized in German. Strange, she had seen a nun walking at almost the same spot when she had first visited Eleonore. There must be a convent nearby. She would ask Frau Meixner.

Eleonore was waiting for Ann in her wheelchair. She

was not wearing a wrapper this time, but a dark skirt and a fluffy white angora sweater. She looked extremely elegant, and Ann was glad she had put on her best twin set of deep wine-red wool.

"You are late," Eleonore said reproachfully after she had greeted Ann. "I was afraid you were not coming after all, so I telephoned just a minute ago. Your landlady answered and said you were on your way. She sounded . . . scared." Eleonore fixed her wide-eyed, innocent gaze on Ann's face. "What would she be scared about?"

"I, er . . ." Ann faltered, color flooding her face. "She did not expect your call."

She realized at once that this explanation made no sense, but Eleonore did not insist. "Really?" she said softly, and began to talk about the books that lay in piles around the bookcase. "The shelves were getting too crammed," she said, "so I spent the whole morning sorting out which ones I don't need any more. I gave several to Trudi. She has a ten-year-old niece who likes to read. I don't know what to do with these." She pointed at a small pile of books with bright covers. "They are for small children. I suppose they will have to be thrown out."

"Oh, no! Don't!" Ann exclaimed, thinking about Minna. "I know someone who would love to have them."

"Your landlady's son?" Eleonore seemed surprised. "Surely he's too big."

"No, not Peter!" Ann giggled at the thought of Peter poring over *Little Red Riding Hood*. She began to tell Eleonore about Minna.

Behind the windows the sun was setting. Trudi came in with the tea tray and lit the lamp under the big pink shade, even though a little daylight still lingered outside.

For the first time in almost forty-eight hours, Ann was

able to relax completely. Ensconced in a comfortable armchair, she sipped the hot sweet tea and savored the delicious little rolled-up waffles filled with apple jam. Even when Eleonore said tentatively, "Trudi told me the Gestapo came yesterday to search your landlady's house. That's why you couldn't come, wasn't it? It must have been very unpleasant." Ann was able to shrug it off with a casual, "Not particularly. They were polite. I think they came by mistake."

Eleonore ignored the last sentence. "You mean they did not find anything?" she asked curiously.

"There was nothing to find." Ann took another waffle.

But Eleonore would not give up. "That's because they did not come at the right time," she said mysteriously. "The best time to find out about things is at night because then people are off guard. They think that as long as it is dark outside nobody can see anything. I've been watching your landlady's attic a good deal these last few nights."

Ann sat up, all her peace gone. She did not want to let Eleonore see how concerned she was, but "Have you seen something special?" slipped off her tongue before she could stop it.

Eleonore nodded gravely. "A few things. As I told you, I don't sleep well and it's easy enough for me to keep awake. On Friday night—I *think* it was Friday. Wait, I have it all written down. Would you bring me my notebook, please?"

Much against her will, Ann got up. "Where is it?"

"See that doll?" Eleonore pointed to a china figurine, about twelve inches high, in a bright pink crinoline, standing on top of the low bookcase. "Just lift her up."

Carefully holding the lady by her tiny waist, Ann lifted

her up. Under the hollow crinoline lay a little volume bound in white leather, a small jeweller's box, and a notebook in mottled covers.

"Here you are," Ann said, handing the notebook to Eleonore and wishing inwardly she could throw it into the fire instead.

"Thanks." Eleonore took the notebook, glanced at Ann and began to laugh. "Goodness, how funny you look! Are you *so* surprised to see that little hiding place of mine? There's nothing secret about it really, but the servants know they must not touch Madame la Marquise. Do you know the song?" She hummed softly, *"Tout va très bien, Madame la Marquise, tout va très bien!"*

There was a long pause, then Eleonore said abruptly, "Everyone has some things that are *very* private. You saw that little white book? It is my diary, and that box . . ." Eleonore swallowed hard. "My mother left it on her dressing table when she went away. Papa gave it to me and said it was Mama's last gift to me. It is a pin, an enameled flower. On the back is engraved, *To my darling daughter to remember me by.* Only I never wear it—and never will! I only keep it because . . . because it is pretty." Eleonore brushed her eyes with a quick movement. "I don't know why I started talking about it," she said petulantly. "Where are my notes?" She picked up the notebook that had slid off her lap onto the carpet and began to flip the pages. "Listen! *October 27th, 1938. At 12:55 a strong light showed in the attic. It moved around.*"

That was when Ilse found me in the attic and Rachel waved the flashlight, Ann thought.

"After a minute or so," Eleonore read on, *"the window was lighted from below as if someone had put the flash-*

light or whatever it was on the floor."

"Yes," breathed Ann. The whole scene came back to her so clearly: the flashlight on the floor, and Ilse hugging Rachel.

"*Yes?*" Eleonore lowered the notebook and stared at Ann. "What do you mean?"

"Yes, no," Ann stammered unhappily, "I only meant that if the window was lighted from below, then . . . the light must have come from below."

Eleonore dropped her lashes. "Certainly. Now the next entry, *1:10 am. Someone was waving the flashlight a minute or two. This could have been a signal.*"

Ann remained silent and Eleonore went on, "*October 28th. Light in the window went out as usual about 9 pm. It went on again at about 11:10, but only for a short time.*"

Because we all went out to look for that briefcase, Ann completed the entry in her mind. She asked nervously, "Is that all?"

Eleonore slammed the notebook shut. "Yes, except for something Trudi told me. On the same night, I mean on the 28th, she and her boyfriend were coming home from a dance. As they passed your house, they saw that boy, Peter, trying to rub out some footsteps in the snow with a broom."

"He must have been playing," Ann mumbled, but Eleonore was not listening. Her face had lit up. "Papa!" she exclaimed.

Colonel Von Waldenfels had come into the room. Very tall and erect in his green military uniform, he walked across the floor with light but firm steps. "It gives me great pleasure to meet you at last, Miss Lindsay," he said, bowing. "I trust your uncle is feeling better?" His En-

109

glish was as perfect as Eleonore's, but Ann did not like his slightly affected tone. Blushing, she murmured something about Uncle Dick feeling quite well but not being out of traction yet.

"Oh, Papa! Ann and I are having such a wonderful time together!" Eleonore exclaimed.

"I can't say how delighted I am to hear it." As he spoke, the colonel bent down and picked up the notebook that had slid to the carpet again. "Writing your memoirs, little girl?" he asked jokingly, glancing at the book and handing it to his daughter. Without waiting for an answer, he took her chin and turned her face toward the lamp.

There was little resemblance between father and daughter, perhaps because their coloring was so different. The colonel's heavy-lidded eyes were ice blue and his close-clipped hair was fair, streaked with white at the temples. But his tone was no longer affected as he said, bending over his daughter's chair, "You look so well, darling! Those new vitamins are doing you good. Or is it the pleasure of Miss Lindsay's company?"

Eleonore rubbed her face against her father's sleeve. "You must call her Ann, Papa, she won't mind. We are great friends."

"Excellent, excellent." The colonel's tone so full of tenderness a minute ago, became affected again. "Maybe . . . er . . . Ann . . . would like to go with you to see *The Magic Flute* next Wednesday? I could order box seats for the matinee. . . ."

"No!" Eleonore cried. "I won't have people see me in a wheelchair."

A little frown of pain appeared on the colonel's forehead. Ann said hastily, "Thank you so much, but I will probably be visiting Uncle Dick on Wednesday after-noon."

"Well . . ." The colonel made a vague gesture and moved toward the door.

Ann immediately began to scramble to her feet. She knew she must leave as soon as possible to avoid further questions from Eleonore. She is too clever for me, Ann thought humbly.

"Are you leaving?" Eleonore asked with disappoint-ment. "But we have so much more to talk about."

"I must, I really must go now," Ann insisted, feeling panicky. "Frau Meixner is expecting me for supper."

"What on earth does it matter whether that woman expects you or not——" Eleonore began haughtily, then bit her lip for the colonel had suddenly reentered the room.

"Now, now, kitten," he admonished. "You can't hold visitors by force, you know! Say good-bye nicely, and start planning another tea party."

"I'll call you and we will decide when to meet next," Eleonore told Ann, rather ungraciously. "But don't for-get the books."

Colonel Von Waldenfels accompanied Ann into the hall, helped her on with her coat and saw her into the elevator. His last words to her were, "Thank you for being a friend to my motherless girl." As he said it, the elevator doors closed, but Ann still had time to see the deep grief on his face. It made her feel guilty because in her mind she had already decided not to see Eleonore again. It was too dangerous. Had the colonel not arrived when he did, Eleonore would have dragged the whole story out of her somehow. The best thing to do would be to think up some good excuse for refusing the next invitation. But *what* excuse? Lying was very difficult.

Ann sighed, and shifted the books so she could see her watch. Only a quarter to five: she had time to deliver the books to Minna. For a minute she toyed with the idea of keeping a few for Rachel; she would enjoy looking at the pictures. But it seemed a little dishonest. She had told Eleonore the books were for Minna and to Minna they must go. Having settled that point, Ann passed by Frau Meixner's house and went to the doctor's.

Minna opened the door. She looked a little less dumpy without the red cloak, but her blue-and-gray-striped dress seemed to have been cut on much the same pattern; a high yoke with thick pleats falling from it. Instead of a rabbit-fur collar, the dress had a lace frill around the throat. It made Minna look as if she had no neck at all.

At first Minna seemed surprised and a little bewildered to see her visitor, then she beamed and said in her childish voice, "Fraulein Anna! Please come in." As she spoke, Minna dropped a quick curtsy which disconcerted Ann so much that her German deserted her. All she could manage was, *"Fur Sie,"* and she dumped the books into Minna's arms.

Minna clutched eagerly at the pile. *"Fur mich? Oh, die Bucher!"* She began to count with her finger, *"Ein, zwei . . . funf!"* Seizing Ann's hand, she said, "Let's go to the parlor and look at them."

Ann followed Minna slowly. The inside of the doctor's house was exactly like Frau Meixner's, only everything was in reverse. The kitchen was on the left of the entrance and the parlor on the right. Instead of Frau Meixner's red plush furniture, Doctor Fromm's parlor was decorated in a vicious bright blue, and there was crochet work everywhere. The doctor had told Ann that the nuns taught Minna how to crochet, but she never imagined there could be so much of it. Crocheted antimacassars perched on the back of every armchair. There were crocheted doilies under the lamps and under every flowerpot on the windowsill. The cushions on the sofa had crocheted covers and even the grandfather clock stood on something that looked like a crocheted mat.

Minna carefully laid the books on the table near the lamp with a crocheted shade. *"Hans Chri - sti - an An - der - sen,"* she spelled out, stroking the picture of the Snow Queen on the cover of one of the books. "Oh, look at that funny boy! Thank you, Fraulein Anna! Thank you so much!"

"They are not from me," Ann said quickly. "They are from Eleonore Von Waldenfels. Remember, we saw her looking from her window?"

Minna nodded gravely. "Yes, I know. I must thank her. She is very kind. Shall we have coffee now? I have baked a cake. It is good . . . mm . . ." She smacked her lips.

"Not now, I'm afraid," Ann said, smiling. "I must get home. Enjoy your books."

She was leaving the parlor when she noticed two large dolls, sitting on chairs on either side of the door. Both wore white crocheted frocks and crocheted hats, one red and the other yellow. Seeing her looking at the dolls, Minna proudly introduced them. "This is Greta," she said, pointing at the yellow-hatted doll, "and that one is Garbo."

"Greta *and* Garbo. Why did you call them that?" Ann asked, trying to suppress a giggle.

"I heard people talking about them," Minna answered indifferently. "Aren't they pretty names?"

"Very pretty," Ann agreed. "Did your brother give you the dolls?"

Minna pouted. "No. Ernst *never* gives me any toys. The sisters gave them to me because I learned my lessons so well and behaved myself. I loved being with the sisters."

She stood on the steps, waving, until Ann disappeared behind the door of Frau Meixner's house.

12

Morritz

"Fraulein Anna, you are not listening to me!" Frau Meixner's voice rose plaintively.

Ann did not answer. She and Frau Meixner were sitting in the kitchen having breakfast and listening to the radio broadcast about the "Martian alarm" in the United States. Staring at the gray wall of fog behind the windows, Ann visualized the panic of millions of people who mistook the radio dramatization of H. G. Wells's *War of the Worlds* for a real event. Apparently people jumped out of windows; got into cars and just drove anywhere; university students fought over the telephone to call their parents to come and take them home.

"Fraulein Anna," Frau Meixner began again, "I want to ask you to do me a favor."

Her mind still on the broadcast, Ann replied vaguely, "I'm sorry, Frau Meixner. Shall I go for the groceries today?"

Frau Meixner looked shocked. *"Nein, nein,* Fraulein Anna. I would not dream of asking you to go out in this weather. If you would just keep an eye on the girls while I am gone—"

Ann jumped up and snapped off the radio. "Of course," she promised readily. "But I really don't mind going out for the groceries if you'd like me to."

"Thank you, but you don't know how to bargain, Fraulein Anna," Frau Meixner answered sadly. "And that bandit of a baker might sell you stale bread again. I will be back in twenty minutes." She rose and went into the hall to get her shopping bag.

Ilse was asleep when Ann went upstairs a few minutes later. She lay flat on her back, breathing unevenly. A half-finished cup of tea stood on the bedside table. Tea and clear soup were still all Ilse could take, to Doctor Fromm's despair. From Ann's room came Rachel's wordless cooing. The child was probably playing with Morritz.

Suddenly there was a loud doggy whimper and an even louder childish cry. Ann rushed across the landing. It took only a glance to establish what had happened. A mesh of Rachel's hair had caught in the buckle of Morritz's collar. In trying to pull apart, dog and child had succeeded only in hurting each other.

"It's all right, it's all right," Ann crooned, kneeling down. "Don't cry, Rachel darling. We'll free you in a jiffy."

But the hair stuck fast. After several attempts, accompanied by growls from Morritz and sobs from Rachel, Ann had to take the collar off and work the hair free with her fingers. "At last!" she breathed, rising. "Hush, Rachel, you'll wake up your sister. Here, give Morritz a good brushing before I put his collar on again."

The brush which Frau Meixner had provided for Morritz's grooming was so large Rachel had to hold it in both hands as she passed it energetically down the dog's back. Ann stood laughing at the pair, with the collar dangling from her hand, and was bending over Morritz to put it on, when she noticed writing on the inner side. Looking closer she deciphered some figures written in black ink. *43190* she made out at last and exclaimed, "Why, it looks like a telephone number!"

Seized by a sudden idea, she dashed into Frau Meixner's bedroom. Ilse was awake now. She looked at Ann dully, and closed her eyes again. "Ilse, Ilse!" Ann shook the girl's shoulder. "Wake up. Look at this. Could it be the telephone number your mother said you could call if you wanted to get in touch with her? Remember, you mentioned that your father wrote it down, but had no time to tell you where."

With what seemed to be a great effort, Ilse raised her head from her pillow. Peering at the collar Ann was dangling in front of her, she murmured, "It is Papa's writing. It could be the number." For a few minutes she became animated. "I must try and call it. Right now, *right now*," she insisted, heaving herself up. "Would you help me downstairs, Anna? I should . . . maybe . . ." The words became more and more blurred and the hand pushing the blanket away clutched Ann's. "I am floating," Ilse whispered. "Hold me down."

"I *am* holding you. Just lie quietly," Ann said soothingly, but Ilse was already asleep. Or was it some kind of stupor? Ann was not sure. Anyway, there seemed to be nothing she could do for Ilse, except one thing—call the number herself.

Stepping softly, she ran downstairs. Frau Meixner was not back yet. So much the better, she decided. Going into the parlor, she lifted the receiver and gave the number to the operator. Standing on tiptoe because the telephone was so high, she waited, all her muscles tense. Somehow, she expected a mysterious whisper to come down the wire. Instead, a young and businesslike voice said in German, "St. Gertrude's convent."

"Er . . ." Ann began, not exactly sure why she was so surprised, "may I speak to Doctor Weiss, please?"

There was a slight gasp at the other end of the wire, and the voice said curtly. "There is no Doctor Weiss here."

"Oh, but please, *please!*" Ann cried, afraid that whoever was speaking would hang up. "I'm not calling for myself, but for Doctor Weiss's daughter, Ilse. She is ill and cannot come to the telephone herself."

"Who is speaking, please?" The voice sounded doubtful and carried an undertone of suspicion.

Ann was not sure whether she should give her name or not, but there seemed to be no harm in it. She said, "Ann Lindsay."

A long pause followed and then, "Frau Oberin wishes to speak to you."

Frau Oberin? Ann guessed it probably meant Mother Superior. There was no time to think about it anyway. Something clicked and a deep guttural voice with a heavy accent asked in English, "Why you call this convent about Doctor Weiss?"

Even in English, it would have been too difficult to

explain about the collar, so Ann simply said, "Doctor Weiss left this telephone number for her family to call if necessary. Her daughter Ilse wanted to talk to her, but she is ill so she asked me to call for her."

Instead of answering, Frau Oberin asked sharply, "You call from England?"

"Oh, no!" Ann exclaimed. "We are here in Frankfurt."

"We?" Frau Oberin sounded alarmed. "The girls here? In Germany?"

"Yes," Ann said.

"Father too?"

"I—we—we don't know."

"Where you live?"

Ann was about to give her address, but thought better of it. She repeated, "We are in Frankfurt," and waited.

A faint chuckle reached her ears and Frau Oberin said, "You know Domkirche? Tomorrow morning you go to early Mass and pray. Take a missal. I come too and pray." The telephone clicked and the line was dead.

Ann knew the Domkirche, or simply the Dom, as the magnificent Gothic church was usually called. She had visited it with Uncle Dick, and she knew exactly how to get there, too. All one had to do was to take the streetcar by the Palmgarten and watch out for a small tobacco shop with a toy bear sitting on top of the door and letting out clouds of tobacco smoke from a cigar. Just beyond the smoking bear there was a stop that would let her out only a short distance away from Old Frankfurt and the Dom.

The question remained: whether or not to tell Frau Meixner. Ann decided against telling. Suppose Frau Meixner became frightened and hysterical and stopped her from going? Later, after it was all over, Ann would tell her. But Ilse must be told at once, before Frau Meixner returned.

Ilse was awake, but when Ann began excitedly, "Ilse, listen, I called that number," she only asked vaguely, "What number?" and began to toss restlessly under the blanket.

She still has a fever, Ann thought, looking at Ilse's parched lips. Rachel, who was nursing her clown, came to the bed and stared at her sister with wide, anxious eyes. Ann watched her pityingly, then, hearing Frau Meixner's steps downstairs, ran to tell her about Ilse.

"I don't know what to do, Fraulein Anna, I really don't," Frau Meixner complained, rubbing her cold hands. "Suppose the Gestapo comes again and Ilse is so sick? It would be impossible to hide her and the child." She left Ann to put the groceries away and went to telephone Doctor Fromm.

He came an hour later, gave Ilse another injection and said she was running a slight temperature. "It is just nerves and fatigue," he said. "All we can do is keep her quiet."

At about two o'clock the telephone rang. To Ann's amazement it was Colonel Von Waldenfels. He sounded apologetic as he asked her to do him a great favor and come in to see Eleonore sometime in the afternoon. "My daughter and I had a . . . a slight disagreement this morning," he explained. "Now she is moping and that is bad for her. Seeing you will cheer her up, even if you can only spare a few minutes. Trudi tells me you left your muffler behind. That makes a good excuse." The colonel laughed, but it sounded somewhat forced.

Ann was not eager to go, but the colonel was so insistent that she reluctantly agreed. One thing was certain, though, she resolved as she was putting on her coat: the minute Eleonore started to talk about the attic, she would leave.

But Eleonore did not look as if she were up to asking any awkward questions. She was lying in her chair, covered to the armpits with a plaid rug. At the sight of Ann, she dabbed her eyes with a rolled-up handkerchief. "Papa said you would be coming to get your muffler," she said. "I am so glad. I feel lonely and . . ." Eleonore's voice began to shake, "Papa has been very unkind to me! He is usually at the barracks till about four, but today he came home before lunch. When he saw me reading a story-book, he became angry and said I was supposed to study in the morning. I tried to explain to him that I felt too tired to bother about history and geography, that an invalid like me could not be expected to keep regular study hours. But he would not listen. He shouted at me! He said I was only tired through laziness, that there was nothing wrong with my head and that from now on he would make sure I studied until a suitable governess can be found. I am *not* lazy, but it is so dull to study by myself."

"It must be rather," Ann agreed. Then, struck by a sudden idea, she suggested, "Couldn't you get in touch with your old classmates? Perhaps a few of them could come here and bring their books. You could all do homework together. That would be fun."

The idea did not arouse Eleonore's enthusiasm. "They did come at first," she said indifferently. "But they soon got tired of it and I wasn't sorry. I didn't particularly care for any of them. One girl continued coming for a long time, though. Once she brought her kitten to show me. I

121

rather liked her. She was a quiet little thing, not noisy like the rest of them. But she turned out to be a *Mischling,* so she had to leave school and of course I could not have her coming here any more."

For a moment, Ann could not imagine what Eleonore was talking about. "A *Mischling?* What do you mean? Oh, I know! The girl was half-Jewish."

Eleonore nodded. "That's right. Don't you think *Mischlings* are even more disgusting than all-Jewish people? Imagine an Aryan taking a Jewish wife, or an Aryan woman married to a Jew. It is *Rassenschande!*"

Ann's color rose. "I don't think it's a racial shame or whatever you call it at all," she retorted. "What really *is* a shame is the way Jewish people are treated and—"

Eleonore interrupted her. "Don't let's quarrel about it," she said. "I have something really funny to tell you. An extraordinary little object came round this morning and presented me with a plate of cakes. Guess who it was."

"Minna Fromm! So that's what she meant when she said she must thank you!"

Eleonore giggled. "Yes, she wanted to thank me for the books. I must say the cakes were very good. I've eaten most of them already. She looked at my things and admired Madame la Marquise a great deal. She really was quite entertaining."

At the mention of Madame la Marquise, Ann felt cold. In another minute Eleonore would produce her notebook and start her cross-examination. She got up hastily.

"Oh, wait a second before you rush off!" Eleonore dived into her pocket and produced a pink envelope. "Read it," she said, handing the envelope to Ann.

Surprised and a little uneasy, Ann tore the envelope

open and drew out a pink card with a lacy border. *You are cordially invited,* she read, *to attend Miss Eleonore Von Waldenfels' birthday party on November 16th. Festive luncheon is to be at noon. It will be followed by a program of entertainment."*

Eleonore's eyes danced as she watched Ann read the invitation. "I wrote it in my best hand," she said. "Aren't you going to RSVP?"

"I could never measure up to your beautiful style," Ann said, in genuine admiration, but as she fingered the pink card she did some quick thinking. Surely it would be quite safe to accept. It seemed extremely unlikely that with other guests present, Eleonore would be able to pursue her detective work.

"I would love to come," she said. "Are there going to be many people?"

"Just you and me. It's going to be our very own, very special party. I am planning all kinds of things and Papa has promised I may have them. Don't forget now, November 16th."

"I won't, but I must run now." Ann stood up resolutely.

Eleonore pouted. "You never really stay. But tell me something: you didn't happen to notice a nun when you arrived? I mean in the street."

Ann shook her head. "Not today, but I have seen a nun in front of this building a couple of times. Why?"

"Nothing. It just seems funny. There is no convent near here, yet Trudi has seen this nun going by and stopping and looking at the house, and yesterday it seems she talked to the doorman. About *me!* She asked him how I was, if I ever went out, if I had been very badly hurt. She told him she knew my mother. I'm sure that's not true."

123

"Why not? She could have been friends with your mother."

"No, she was not. I don't remember any nuns ever coming to see Mother. And I don't like people asking about me."

Eleonore was not the only one concerned about the mysterious nun. When Ann came out of the elevator she saw Colonel Von Waldenfels standing in the lobby, talking to the doorman.

"You say she was here again, walking up and down outside, only a few minutes ago?" he was saying. "Did you notice in which direction she went? I see—"

As Ann reached the door, she saw the colonel's powerful Mercedes Benz pull away from the curb.

13

Frau Oberin

The kitchen clock said a quarter past six when Ann propped a note, *Gone to church,* against the coffeepot where Frau Meixner was bound to see it when she got up. Whether she would believe it was another matter, but at least it was the truth.

The streetcar was cold and drafty. Ann sat in a corner clutching her ticket in one hand, a missal in the other. It was lucky she had been able to find a missal on the shelf in Frau Meixner's parlor because she did not own one. The missal was old, with greenish spots on the cover, and it was full of dried flowers, little religious cards and paper bookmarks. An inscription in yellowed ink on the flyleaf said, *To Wilhelmina* and the date *1854.* Ann wondered whether the unknown Wilhelmina was a relative of Frau Meixner. She imagined her as a little girl in pantalettes, trotting off to Mass.

"Domkirche!" the conductor shouted.

Ann jumped up and dropped the missal, scattering small pictures and dried flowers in all directions. Scarlet, she picked them up, crushing a few flowers to smithereens, and hastily thrust them all back into the book. The conductor looked relieved when she finally managed to get off.

Standing on the pavement, she shivered with cold. She liked the old part of Frankfurt, but now, with shop windows barred and shuttered and a bitter north wind whistling around the corners, the streets did not look quaint, only desolate. The Domkirche loomed not far away, its spire piercing the milky-white sky.

Ann began to walk toward the cathedral. Her knees shook a little as she opened the heavy door. The early service had not started yet, and the church was lit only by a few candles. At first glance it seemed almost empty, but when Ann's eyes became accustomed to the semidarkness she could make out a figure in a black habit sitting in the fifth row of the benches. With quickened breath, she began to move down the aisle. She was just a few steps away from the black habit when she realized there were four other nuns in the second row. Which one would be Frau Oberin? Before she could decide what to do, a barely audible whisper ordered, "Sit down. Open book."

Startled, Ann sat down and fumbled with her gloves. Stuffing them into her pocket, she opened the missal at random, and waited. Nothing happened and at last she dared to glance at the black-veiled figure. She had once seen a painting of a nun's face, shown against a stained-glass window. It was a beautiful face, the eyelids

126

dropped, peace in every feature. The painting was called *Serenity*. Frau Oberin was quite different. The black veil framed the broad face of a middle-aged peasant woman with shrewd gray eyes and a square stubborn chin. There was nothing serene about Frau Oberin. On the contrary, she seemed forceful and nervously alert.

When Ann began to whisper in German, "Ilse is very ill. If she had news of her mother, it might—" Frau Oberin cut her short. "Don't look at me," she ordered. "Look at your book so people will think you are praying."

The handful that made up the congregation was several rows in front of them, but all the same Ann realized they had to be careful. She bent her head over her missal.

Frau Oberin began to thumb through the pages of her own prayer book. Ann heard, *"Mutter of Gottes . . ."* and then, still in German, "Ilse? Is that the older girl? She is ill?"

"Doctor Fromm says it is nervous exhaustion," Ann whispered back.

"So. And the little girl?"

Ann hesitated. Should she tell about Rachel's loss of speech? She decided it would be better for this sensible, shrewd woman to know the whole story.

Frau Oberin sighed. "Poor child. Well, we once had a nun who became so frightened when lightning struck a tree in front of her cell window that she could not talk any more. Two years later, a fire broke out in the convent, and she regained her speech. Please God, the same may happen to the little girl."

"Oh, I hope so!" Ann whispered eagerly.

This seemed like a good opportunity to ask the question uppermost in her mind. "Frau Oberin, is *she,* I mean the mother, in your convent?"

127

Frau Oberin raised her bowed head. The gray eyes surveyed Ann's face critically. Then her lips formed "Yes."

"But what would happen if the convent were searched, like Frau Meixner's house?"

"*They* may come, but they won't get her." Frau Oberin spoke with absolute certainty. Ann began to understand why Doctor Weiss had chosen St. Gertrude's convent for a refuge.

The choir boys appeared with a rustle of robes, and flames sprang from the big candles at the altar. More people had come in. The church was filled with the sounds of footsteps and murmurs of prayers. Frau Oberin took a rosary from her pocket. Her voice was so low now that Ann could get only the gist of what she was saying, but that was enough for her to grasp the situation. St. Gertrude's order had a branch in Switzerland near Zurich where they maintained a small rest home for sisters convalescing after illness. Frau Oberin was planning to send Doctor Weiss there, disguised as a nun. She could not cross the border under her own name of course, but there was a man who had promised to provide a false passport. The trouble was that he charged a high price for such a dangerous job, and the money had still to be found. Doctor Weiss had a pearl pin with her when she arrived, and one of the novices had given it to her uncle, who was a jeweller, without telling him to whom the pin belonged. Now he was trying to sell it. Doctor Weiss was sure her husband and daughters were either in Switzerland or already in England, so she was biding her time, thinking it would be better to let things calm down before trying to join them. Now, of course, everything was different. New plans would have to be made to save the girls as well. It seemed hopeless to try and do anything for Herr Weiss. One could only pray for him.

The service started. Frau Oberin put her rosary into her pocket. Under cover of the prayers, she asked for Ann's telephone number. "But not the house where you are living," she cautioned. "Too dangerous now. Have you some other place where we could reach you with a message?"

Rather hesitantly, Ann gave Uncle Dick's hospital number. There was no choice and, besides, she was planning to tell him everything right after the service.

With an almost imperceptible movement of her head, Frau Oberin indicated to Ann that the conversation was over.

The service was not a long one, and half an hour later, Ann was threading her way out in the wake of the congregation. Frau Oberin remained in her seat, rosary beads clicking in her hands again.

After the heady smell of incense and candle wax, the cold morning air felt exhilarating. Ann walked briskly, jiggling the change in her pocket and congratulating herself that her meeting with Frau Oberin had escaped notice. No one had given her a glance.

Then suddenly her feeling of security vanished. Someone behind her was calling, "Fraulein Anna! Fraulein Anna!" and suppressing an impulse to run and lose herself in the rapidly increasing throng of people, Ann turned around. Minna Fromm came running up, looking more oddly-shaped than ever in her red velvet cloak. "You dropped this!" she panted, reaching Ann and handing her a lacy paper bookmark with a pressed violet glued at one end.

"Thank you," Ann said, taking it and hoping that

129

Minna would go on her way, but the chubby figure kept on trotting beside her. "I like coming to Domkirche," Minna chattered. "Ernst gives me money for the street-car and for the collection box, but today I did not know which coin was for the box and which for going home. And then I saw you! And then that thing flew out of your book."

So Minna had not necessarily seen her with Frau Oberin. Trying to sound offhand, Ann asked, "Where were you sitting? I didn't see you."

Minna seemed surprised by the question. "Sitting? In the front, of course! I like to see the candles and the flowers and the boys in their red dresses. But I looked back and saw you with Frau Oberin. I wanted to wave but Frau Oberin never allowed us to wave in church. Ooh, she was so strict!" Minna's eyes became quite round as she peered at Ann from beneath her tam-o'-shanter. "Then the priest rang his little bell and that means bow-your-head-and-pray." Minna said the last words in one gulp, showing that the instructions she had received in the convent were well and truly remembered.

Ann breathed again. Minna could not possibly have overheard a word from the front row, but all the same a nagging voice in the back of her mind kept repeating, "It's a pity she saw you with Frau Oberin. She might talk about it to someone."

A sudden longing to tell everything to someone who would understand, made her say to Minna, "Here's your streetcar. Hop in. I'm not going back to Mylius Strasse yet. I want to visit my uncle."

It was still too early for visitors, but the receptionist now knew Ann by sight and let her in. To her surprise and pleasure she found the alarming and cumbersome traction apparatus gone. Uncle Dick was sitting up in bed. From the position of his eyebrows, however, she could see he was not in the best of moods. A sheet of paper covered with penciled numbers lay before him.

This time she made sure the door was closed, before beginning, "Uncle Dick! I have a whole lot of things to tell you. . . ."

As before, he listened to her story without interrupting, but Ann could not help noticing that his face became curiously set as she went on. However, when she had finished, he only said, "Wait! Let me collect my thoughts and get all this straight. No, don't say anything. Just answer my questions. You found a telephone number on the dog's collar, and you called it—just like that?"

"Yes. Why not?"

"Did it never occur to you," he asked in a carefully controlled voice, "that the number might *not* have been the one Doctor Weiss gave to her husband?"

"But it had to be," Ann explained. "Ilse said it was her father's writing."

"A few figures, which you yourself say were half washed out by the snow? And Ilse, according to your own description, semidelirious? Don't you realize that when you called that number you might have been calling the *Gestapo?*"

Ann stared at him, appalled. "But—but—" she began.

"Look," he said, suddenly sounding very tired. "Let me explain it to you. From what I gather, someone in the Gestapo was supplying Doctor Weiss with release papers to get Jews out of concentration camps. Right?"

Ann nodded.

"Fine. Now, isn't it obvious that Doctor Weiss would

131

not go to Gestapo headquarters every time she needed to speak to that man? So there must have been a telephone number she could call—if not regularly, then at least in case of emergency. It's also possible—no, *probable*—that they used some kind of a code when they communicated. But now that the Gestapo chiefs suspect that someone in their organization has betrayed them, all the telephone lines are undoubtedly being monitored. And *you* called and asked pointblank about Doctor Weiss. . . ."

"I'm sorry," Ann whispered miserably.

"Never mind. You were lucky this time and anyway all this will be over shortly."

"Over?" Ann choked. "You *are* sending me back to England after all?"

"No. We're both leaving. I was planning to go next Monday, but Doctor Fromm insists I need further treatment. I tried to dissuade him—goodness knows, the hospital bill is large enough already—but he's adamant. So I've made plane reservations for November the seventeenth. The car will be sent over later. Doctor Fromm says I should not drive for at least a month more."

November the seventeenth. It seemed to Ann that the words stared at her from every shop sign as she sat in the streetcar on the way back to Mylius Strasse. It meant only a little over two weeks, and from the look on the Mother Superior's face it had been clear that getting false passports might take a long time. . . .

Doctor Fromm was of the same opinion. He was examining Ilse when Ann came home and she told him and Frau Meixner about her meeting with Frau Oberin. "Goodness only knows how long it will take the good Mother to get those passports and, more important, the money to pay for them," he said, frowning and sitting heavily down on the nearest kitchen chair. "My funds are less than modest. Minna is provided for—my stepmother left her a substantial amount of money in trust, and the house is in her name. But for myself—" He sighed.

Frau Meixner was rubbing her eyes with her apron. "Those poor children have no chance," she murmured. "I hoped and hoped their mother was already abroad and would be able to do something to save them. But she is in hiding herself. What is going to happen now?"

"Ah, what can I say! We must wait and see." The doctor rose to go, and Ann had to help him to put on his coat because he kept missing the sleeves.

14

"We repeat the first bulletin..."

It seemed to Ann that waiting was all that anyone did for the next few days. Something was going to happen, she was sure of it, and she knew that Frau Meixner and Doctor Fromm had the same feeling. The "something" was shapeless and vague and terribly frightening. Even little Rachel looked as if she was affected by that strange, gnawing foreboding. She hardly played with Morritz any more, but just sat quietly, her arms around his neck, starting each time someone came into the room.

Only Ilse knew exactly what *she* was waiting for. Sitting up in bed, propped on pillows, waxlike skin drawn tight across her cheekbones, she kept her eyes fixed on Frau Meixner's little bronze clock. "I know that the Gestapo will be coming again," she told Ann. "I watch the time and I think, 'They did not come at ten, but they might come at five past.' And so it goes, hour after hour, and it is killing me, bit by bit. If it were not for Rachel, I would almost wish the Gestapo *would* come and take me. Anything is better than waiting for them."

"Don't think about it," Ann begged, frightened by the wild look in Ilse's eyes. "Think how wonderful it is that we have found where your mother is and that you will see her again. Soon maybe." And as Ilse kept silent, she asked, trying not to show her mounting irritation, "Don't you want to see your mother? I thought you would be delirious with joy when Doctor Fromm told you the news."

Ilse's lips began to tremble. "No, no! It is not like that at all," she said. "I worship Mama. Only she seems so far away and besides . . ." her lips trembled even more, "I can't help wondering why she doesn't get in touch with us, now that she knows where we are."

"She may not know it," Ann said quickly. "I'm not at all sure Frau Oberin intended telling her, and even supposing she did, it would be too dangerous for your mother to write or to call."

"Yes," Ilse agreed listlessly, "it would be too dangerous."

Walking to the window, Ann leaned on the sill and cupped her chin in her hands. Maybe Doctor Weiss was watching the clock too and expecting the Gestapo to raid the convent. It could happen . . . it could happen easily. Frau Oberin realized it. Ann remembered the stubborn look on her face, the rigid fingers turning the pages of the prayer book. Uncle Dick was probably anxious too. And— startled by a sudden thought, Ann straightened up. For the first time, it occurred to her that beyond all the houses and gardens and streets that separated Mylius Strasse from the center of the city, somewhere in Gestapo headquarters, the man who had helped Doctor Weiss to save the Jews was waiting to be discovered at any moment. Was he sitting at a desk, or, like Ann, standing by the window watching small white clouds chase each other all over the gray November sky?

Heavy shoes clattered across the landing. Ilse stirred in her bed. "Who is it?" she whispered, her wide gaze fixed anxiously on the door.

"It's only Peter," Ann reassured her, turning away from the window and coming to the bed. "Funny, I wonder why he's back from school at this time. He seems to be coming home earlier and earlier these last few days. Frau Meixner has noticed it too."

The reason for Peter's early homecoming was discovered next morning. The headmaster called and said that Peter had not been in school since Tuesday. It was now Friday. He had missed almost a week. Was he sick?

Bewildered and upset, Frau Meixner muttered something about Peter not having been well but that he would be back to school on Monday. Then she sat down in the kitchen to wait for the culprit's return.

Ann expected a stormy scene, but when Frau Meixner saw her son slide cautiously through the back door, she only buried her face in the kitchen towel and began to sob.

This seemed to disconcert Peter who stood swinging his school bags and measuring with his eye the distance between the door and the stairs.

"You terrible, terrible boy," Frau Meixner got out at last. "Where have you been?"

136

Peter's chin went up. "Gruneburg Park," he muttered, defiantly.

Ann, who was peeling potatoes at the sink, put her knife down and shivered. The weather had been very cold all week. To think that Peter had sat outside for hours every day!

At the word "park" Frau Meixner sat up. "I suppose you were playing football with street urchins. Is that it? Or climbing trees? And here am I thinking you are safe at school."

Peter came closer. "I did not go to the park to play," he said. "I just sat on a bench and froze. But I liked it better than going to school. I hate it. The whole class knows the Gestapo searched our house. Now no one wants to sit with me, and the boys whisper among themselves and give me looks. They don't trust me any more."

Without waiting for his mother's answer, he turned around and raced up the stairs.

"That is what happens when there is no man in the house," Frau Meixner sobbed. "I should take a strap to that boy, but I have no heart to punish him. But he has to go back. Maybe Doctor Fromm can talk some sense into him."

The doctor came that evening and talked to Peter for a long time behind closed doors. On Monday Peter went to school. His parting words were, "All right. I am going because Doctor Fromm says I can't be an engineer if I don't study. But I won't stand for those boys whispering behind my back and pushing me on the sly when we play games. Next time it happens, I'm going to *sock* them."

He was barely out of the door when Eleonore telephoned. "I was going to call you yesterday," she told

Ann, "but it was Sunday and I thought you might be in church." A slight pause followed and Eleonore added, "I didn't know you were Roman Catholic."

"I'm not."

Ann would have given anything to recall the words, but they were already out. Why, oh, why, was it so hard to lie!

"*Not* Roman Catholic?" Eleonore's surprise sounded exaggerated. "That's funny. Trudi met that Minna What's-her-name at the baker's and she told her you were both at Domkirche. Were you just sightseeing?"

"Yes, that's right," Ann said, wishing Eleonore would stop questioning her this way.

Eleonore chuckled lightly. "During Mass? Well, that's not really what I wanted to talk to you about. Do you know," she lowered her voice, "that that boy, Peter, walks a dog in your garden every morning and keeps looking around as if he were afraid to be seen with it?"

"A dog? Yes—yes, I know . . ." Ann stammered unhappily. "It—it belongs to someone in the block. Peter just walks it."

"Before anyone is awake?" Ann could almost see Eleonore shrug her shoulders. But she did not pursue the subject and went on gaily, "It's not that, either, that I'm calling about, though. I've had a wonderful idea about my party. Would you please come at eleven instead of twelve? We shall open my presents together! Papa always gives me lovely things and I have two aunts in Munich who usually remember my birthday. I won't touch anything until you arrive. Promise to come early?"

"Yes, of course. Of course I'll promise. At eleven. On the sixteenth. Goodbye." Ann slowly put the receiver back on its hook. So Minna *had* talked. The story that

138

had reached Eleonore was not strictly accurate—she hadn't been with Minna until afterward—and apparently Minna had not mentioned Frau Oberin . . . or had she?

Across the hall, Ann could see Frau Meixner standing by the ironing board, a big basket of washing on the floor beside her. Feeling too downhearted to talk, Ann passed through the kitchen without saying a word and went upstairs. She had not reached the landing when Frau Meixner's voice reached her.

Something must be very wrong because for the first time instead of the ceremonious "Fraulein Anna," Frau Meixner was calling, "Anna! Anna! *Kommen Sie!*"

Ann rushed downstairs.

At first glance everything seemed normal. The kitchen was warm and peaceful. The washing in the basket, stiff from drying in the frosty air outside, smelled of yellow soap, and the small radio played soft music. But there was terror on Frau Meixner's face and her hand holding the iron was shaking. "Listen, listen," she whispered, pointing at the radio. "They are going to say it again."

The music stopped. A short pause followed and then the announcer said, "We repeat the first bulletin. Baron Von Rath, a young attaché at the German Embassy in Paris, has just been shot by a Jewish murderer. His condition is critical."

15

The Crystal Night

Minutes after the radio announcement, the telephone started to ring. The first call came from Doctor Fromm. He had to make it brief because Frau Meixner could hardly hold the receiver in her shaking hand. The doctor only said that the persecution of Jews was bound to be worse than ever and that it was important to be very careful.

"Careful!" Frau Meixner said bitterly, pouring herself a cup of coffee and spilling most of it into the saucer. "Of course we are careful, but the first time the Gestapo came we were warned, and now . . ." She began to drink the coffee, her teeth chattering against the cup.

The second call came from Peter's godmother in Offenbach. She simply wanted to talk about the "terrible news." Frau Meixner was obviously in no state to talk about anything, so Ann had to speak to her. She tried to explain that Frau Meixner was not feeling well and would telephone tomorrow, but Frau Lemke kept on talking about a Jewish family across the street from her, how scared they were and how the Fuhrer was sending his own physician, Doctor Brandt, to Paris.

Uncle Dick's call was the last. He sounded tense and worried. "Mind what you say and do," he told Ann. "This is a highly dangerous situation. A nurse came in a minute ago and said that Von Rath is not expected to live. It's going to be rough on the Jews here if, or rather when, he dies." And with a final, "Don't do anything foolish," Uncle Dick rang off.

Declaring that she was too nervous to cook, Frau Meixner made sandwiches for lunch and again for supper. Peter took his upstairs and used them to lure Morritz away from Rachel and into his room. When Ann went upstairs, Rachel was weeping, and Ilse, looking paler than ever, kept asking, "Why does Frau Meixner look so upset? What has happened?"

Ann muttered something vague and escaped. Frau Meixner had asked her not to tell Ilse anything, hoping the girl might have a peaceful night.

Frau Meixner herself spent the night in the kitchen. She had brought in an armchair from the parlor and sat wrapped in a warm robe, listening to the radio and dozing off between bulletins. The radio was turned low, but Ann could hear its muffled sound all through the night.

At seven in the morning, Frau Meixner, gray-faced and heavy-eyed, went upstairs to bathe and dress, while Ann took her place by the radio. The news was not encouraging. Von Rath was sinking rapidly, and, between the bulletins, there were hysterical accusations against the Jewish population—the assassination of Von Rath was only part of a Jewish plot to destroy all Aryans in Germany—more assassinations would follow if measures were not taken. . . .

Ann knew the whole story by heart now. A young Jewish boy named Herschel Grynzpan had been sent to Paris some time previously by his parents, who thought he would be safer in France than in Germany. When he learned that his family had been brutally treated and then deported to Poland, together with other Polish-born Jews, he decided to avenge them by killing the German ambassador. But he could not reach the ambassador. Instead, he was ushered into the office of the third secretary, Ernst von Rath.

Ann knew that, unwittingly, the young man had played into the Nazis' hands, and that now they had the excuse they wanted for full-scale persecution of Jews. She would have liked to go over to the hospital and discuss it all with Uncle Dick, but his orders had been firm: "Keep off the streets. As soon as Von Rath dies, demonstrations will begin and . . . reprisals too."

So Ann stayed by the radio the whole day, listening to the music, to news about the Metro strike in France . . . the Dionne quintuplets' first train ride . . . Pope Pius XI's illness . . . more music . . . the weather forecasts . . . holding her breath every time a further announcement came. "According to the latest bulletin received from France, Baron Von Rath's condition remains critical. Doctors are still pessimistic about his chances."

Every half hour or so, Frau Meixner would come in

and ask, "Fraulein Anna, any news?" and Ann would answer, "He is still alive."

But toward evening, the chorus of children singing on the radio stopped abruptly. Ann knew that Von Rath had died even before the announcement was made.

She turned the radio off. There was no further need for it. Frau Meixner, who was in the kitchen with her, became ashen and whispered, "Terrible things will happen now, Fraulein Anna. Mark my words."

But the night and the following morning passed quietly enough. In the afternoon, the radio announced that crowds of demonstrators were gathering in the streets, "to express their indignation against the Jewish assassins," but Mylius Strasse remained peaceful.

Ilse knew what was happening now and, to Frau Meixner's surprise, instead of being frightened she began to feel better.

"Nothing strange about it," Doctor Fromm commented when he came in to see them. "Before, Ilse felt that the danger was directed at her and Rachel. Now the entire Jewish population is threatened. There is safety in numbers and that is a relief to her. Thank God for that at least!"

Peter, who had been very quiet for the last couple of days, was now in a state of great excitement and kept dashing out of doors "to see how things are going."

"Some of the big boys have made fire bombs," he confided to Ann. "They are going to throw them at Jewish stores."

Shocked, Ann almost dropped the cup of cocoa she was taking upstairs to Ilse. "And you think it is *fun?*" she asked indignantly, wiping the spilled cocoa off the table.

143

"Don't you realize that all Jews cannot be held responsible for what one person has done?"

"Well, I suppose so," Peter agreed halfheartedly. "But you should see those bombs fly! First there is a hiss-sh-sh, and then boo-oom!" He pretended to throw a bomb and his face glowed.

As soon as dusk fell, little knots of people began to gather, even in quiet Mylius Strasse. Watching from behind the curtains of the dark parlor, Ann saw half a dozen young men going from group to group, talking and gesturing. More and more people came. There was no shouting, but a low angry hum that became louder every minute. The street lights went on, and as if that were a signal, the shapeless crowd sorted itself out, formed ranks and marched off in the direction of Feldberg Strasse.

Ann pulled the curtains farther back and pressed her face against the glass. As far as she could see, the street was now deserted. She was just stepping back when the sound of an explosion shook the windowpanes. A distant roar of voices followed and several people appeared in the street, running and calling to each other.

Ann dropped the curtain. A cold numbness was slowly spreading from the back of her neck and down her spine. For several minutes, she remained standing in the middle of the room, her frightened imagination leaping, building up terrors. She thought she could already see Frau Meixner's house surrounded by people, faces peering through the windows, hands forcing the door, ransacking, grabbing the Jewish girls, maybe killing them. . . .

The telephone rang and she was glad because it chased the dreadful visions away. It was Doctor Fromm. He wanted to make sure Peter was safely at home. "The Jewish delicatessen in Feldberg Strasse is burning," he said.

144

"Someone has thrown an incendiary bomb and looting is going on. I saw a group of boys and one looked like Peter, but they ran away before I could get close enough to see properly."

"I'm sure he is here," Ann answered, "but I'll check of course and—"

"Fraulein Anna! Fraulein Anna!" Frau Meixner came running into the parlor. "Peter is gone! I told him again and again not to go out, but when does he listen?"

"Peter's gone," Ann informed the doctor hastily. "I can't talk now."

"I must go after him and get him back!" Frau Meixner cried distractedly, running into the hall for her coat, then coming back to Ann. "His jacket is gone and his earmuff cap. I heard the back door close about ten minutes ago, but I was busy with the girls and I did not pay much attention."

Ann looked at Frau Meixner's anguished face, tears channeling down her powdered cheeks, and felt sorry for her. "Let *me* go after Peter," she offered. "He must be in Feldberg Strasse watching the fire with the other boys. It will only take me a minute to run there and get him."

"Oh, Fraulein Anna! But your uncle said you mustn't go out. You will take care of yourself, won't you?" Frau Meixner waved her hands, still crying and blaming herself and Peter in equal parts for his disobedience, and swearing to lock him in his room if he ever got back.

Ann threw on her coat, tied a scarf on her head and ran out of the house. She was going down the steps when she saw two of Peter's classmates she knew by sight rush by. "Have you seen Peter?" she called after them.

One of the boys hurried on without answering, but the other called over his shoulder, "He went that way," and

145

pointed in the direction of Gruneberg Weg.

Ann paused for a moment to think. A group of men jostled her as they passed and she heard them talking about Kaiser Strasse. It occurred to her that Peter might well have decided to go and see the demonstrations in the center of the city. If he had, he would have taken the streetcar in Eschersheim Landstrasse. Maybe she could catch up with him there. Ann took a deep breath and broke into a steady run.

There was quite a crowd waiting for the streetcar, but almost immediately Ann spotted the familiar small figure in a blue plaid jacket, too tight across the shoulders, and the red earmuff cap. She began to thread her way toward Peter, but at that moment the streetcar arrived and everybody tried to get on at the same time. Ann hurried forward but, to her dismay, Peter had already vanished inside. She scrambled desperately and managed to get on too but the streetcar was packed and she was forced to stand on the landing.

Pressed against a hard metal projection, Ann stood on tiptoe, trying to look over the shoulders of the people standing in front of her. She must not miss Peter getting off, she thought as the lighted shop windows, street lamps, and the crowded pavements flashed past.

After several stops, a stout woman who was blocking Ann's view began to scramble off, dropping parcels in all directions. Someone must have picked them up for her because she said, *"Danke schon."* Craning forward, Ann saw it was Peter, and he was getting off. With a desperate, *"Entschuldigen Sie, bitte,"* she hurled herself across the landing and managed to jump off just as the streetcar began to move.

146

The first thing she noticed, as she tried to get her bearings, was the red glow spreading across the sky. More shops on fire?

But there was no time to think about it now, for she must find Peter. She looked around and saw him, strolling along ahead of her, his red cap appearing and disappearing in the crowd. She hurried after him, but it was difficult to move in the throng and she could not seem to catch up with him. People were gathering from every direction, some grim, some excited. Everyone was shouting and waving. Ann was puzzled by a strange silvery sound that seemed to come from somewhere quite close and was steadily increasing in volume. The clouds above her head were now fiery red. Soon the whole sky was ablaze, making the street lights almost invisible.

Someone screamed, "The synagogues are burning!" and a young girl walking beside Ann buried her face in the collar of her coat. Could she be Jewish? Ann thought fleetingly. Out in *this?* But she was gaining on Peter now. The red cap bobbed only a few steps away.

She was just getting ready to shout to him when a human wave suddenly surged forward, carrying her around the next corner and flinging her against a lamppost. She felt her feet slipping and, as she staggered and fell, she instinctively flung out her arms to save herself. Pain cut like a knife across her palms.

With an immense effort, she pulled herself up, clutching at the lamppost. Blood was streaming from her hands. She touched the ragged wound on the palm of her left hand and a piece of glass fell out. It was only then that she realized that the glistening stuff on the ground was glass from the broken shop windows. There were mounds of it. Pulling out her handkerchief, she wrapped it around the wound. Her right hand would have to take care of itself.

Still carried along by the crowd, she gave up all hope of finding Peter. The street was filled with acrid smoke, and hundreds of S.A. men, in brown uniforms with swastikas on their sleeves, were running, waving flaming torches. As Ann watched the reflection of the red and blue flames dance in the plate-glass window of a big store, she suddenly saw them waver and become distorted as the glass collapsed with that strange silvery sound she had heard before.

Several Nazi youths hurled themselves through the gaping hole. Bales of cloth flew out and piled up on the street. Shelves torn off the walls followed, then boards from the counters. One boy flung his torch into the middle of the pile, another followed suit. In a few seconds the whole pile was ablaze. People gathered around and burst into song. Ann could not understand all the words, but she did make out something about "cutting the Jews' throats."

She tried to escape, but it was difficult because the crowd was now dancing around the fire, its red glow illuminating faces and cavorting figures, and making Ann feel she was in the middle of some nightmarish dream. An elderly woman poked her in the ribs, "Sing, madchen, sing," she urged. "We are going to smoke those Jewish rats out of the city." With the last words, she bent down and deftly extracted from the bonfire a large piece of silk that the flames had not reached yet. Glancing furtively round, she stuffed the silk under her coat.

Something exploded nearby and a child screamed. Ann saw a well-dressed young couple standing not far away from her. The man had a small girl in his arms. The child was crying and hiding her face in his shoulder. "Don't cry," the man admonished. "Look. This is history."

"Let's go around the other side and see some more," the young woman suggested.

Suddenly, Ann was not terrified any more, just sickened. She knew that at all costs, she had to get out of that yelling, singing, dancing crowd. Coughing, half blinded by smoke, she began to fight her way out, diving under elbows, shoving with her shoulders, even clawing at the hands that tried to push her away.

She got through somehow and started to run toward the nearest corner, stepping over the piles of broken glass, falling, scrambling up again, colliding with people and still running through the blinding haze of the bonfires.

Panting, her coat torn, her stockings in shreds, she reached a side street and stopped to get her breath. There was not so much broken glass here and less smoke, but it was crowded too, only it was a different crowd from that in the Kaiser Strasse. There, the Nazis were acting as avenging angels, protecting Germany from the "Jewish Peril." Here, behind the stage, they were openly and avidly looting. A group of brown-shirted youths surrounded the broken window of a jeweler's. One was scooping up earrings, pins, and cufflinks, and throwing them in handfuls to his comrades. A little farther back, not daring to come too close, the crowd waited, watching anxiously for a stray piece of jewelry, hands outstretched, ready to pounce. Nearby, a food shop was being looted, but in a more businesslike way. Without singing or shouting, in fact in almost total silence, men, women and even children stuffed their bags with groceries, threw the bags over their shoulders and disappeared into the night.

Feeling utterly exhausted and a little dizzy, Ann moved on. She was not exactly sure of her whereabouts now, but her aim was to get away from the center of the city and find a streetcar stop. The thought made her put her hand into her coat pocket. Her purse was gone. She must have dropped it somehow or it had been stolen. It was not much of a loss, only one mark and some small change, but the mere thought of trying to get back to Mylius Strasse on foot made her feel faint. She set her teeth and plodded on in what she hoped was the right direction.

She was crossing the street when two teen-age girls catapulted out of a store, fighting over a gold evening bag with a jewelled clasp. "I want it. Hans is taking me out tomorrow night," one hissed, tugging at the bag. The other girl snarled something and pulled. The bag tore in two and the girls fell apart so violently that they almost pushed Ann off the curb.

She regained her balance somehow, but the jolt made the scratches on her palms bleed again, and her handkerchief had disappeared. Sticking her hands into her pockets, Ann was about to resume walking, when she heard hobnailed shoes pounding behind her and Peter's voice shouting, "Fraulein Anna! Wait for me!"

"Peter!" Ann cried. "Goodness! I've been looking for you everywhere! Your mother is out of her mind with worry about you!"

Peter glared at Ann from under the red cap. "Why should Mutti be worried? I can take care of myself. All the boys in our street went to see the fun. There was no reason for me not to go too."

"All right," Ann said bluntly, "so now you've seen the fun. How did you like it?"

Peter's eyelids dropped. He shouted, "I don't know!" and kicked the nearest lamppost. After a short silence, he said, without looking at Ann, "I talked to a boy. . . . His home is near Judenstrasse. That is where a lot of Jews live. He said that people had gone into the Jewish houses and thrown small children out of their beds. Then they dragged the beds outside and set fire to them." He waited for an answer and as Ann kept her lips set tightly together, he tugged at her sleeve, "Why don't you say something?"

Ann swallowed. It would be difficult to explain to Peter that the pain in her hands and her aching bones had dimmed in her mind the scenes of arson and plunder she had seen. Now his story brought it all back again and made her too sick to speak. "I don't think there is anything for me to say," she answered at last. "You know the answer yourself."

Peter only shrugged his shoulders and strode on, his hands in the pockets of his jacket. Something jingled and Ann stopped short. "Peter! Do you have any money? Enough to get us home?"

Without speaking, Peter held out his palm with a few coins on it.

Ann counted the money carefully, then she counted it a second time. Almost, but not quite enough for two. Feeling ready to cry, she felt the hem of her coat. There was a hole in her pocket she had neglected to repair. Maybe a coin had slipped through. . . . It had! Ann ripped the hem, and held it to the light. Just enough! "Let's go to the nearest stop," she told Peter. "You lead."

16

Herr Weiss

"Wake up, Fraulein Anna! It is almost ten and your uncle wants you on the telephone!" Frau Meixner punctuated every word with a bang on the door. Ann raised her head from the pillow and called back in a sleepy voice, "Yes, yes, I'm coming."

She lost her slippers twice while descending the stairs because she was still only half awake. Seizing the receiver, she mumbled, "Hello, Uncle Dick," and hoped she was not going to fall asleep standing up. Her uncle's voice, brisk as usual but with a note of tension in it, made her feel instantly wide awake. "How are you after your experiences last night?" Uncle Dick asked. "Frau Meixner told me. Just feeling tired? Well, unless you're really collapsing, I want you to come over to the hospital as soon as possible. Something unexpected has come up."

He refused to discuss anything further on the telephone and rang off.

Frau Meixner looked apprehensive when Ann told her about this conversation. "Something must be wrong," she murmured. "Fraulein Anna, you had better hurry."

Ann did hurry. She gulped down her breakfast and ran all the way to the streetcar stop. The day was mild and foggy, and when the streetcar arrived at last its windows were covered with a fine mist. She dabbed at it with her glove, thinking meanwhile that Frau Meixner could be right. Maybe something was wrong. But what?

Frowning, she peered through the clear spot she had made on the glass. Wreckage from the night before lay everywhere, and here and there the remains of bonfires still smouldered. Gaping shop fronts opened onto empty and blackened interiors. Piles of splintered glass lay in the gutters. As the streetcar slowed down at a crossroads, she noticed a big leather goods shop whose facade was still intact. A nun was standing in front of it, holding a collection box, and next to her a tall man was studying the array of leather briefcases and gloves in the window. Colonel Von Waldenfels! Ann was sure of it, even though his back was turned to her. Was it simply a coincidence? Or was he talking to the nun as she had talked to Frau Oberin in Domkirche, doing it in such a way it would not be noticed?

The streetcar moved on and the nun and the tall man in the military coat disappeared from Ann's sight.

Doctor Fromm was waiting for her in front of the hospital. He was obviously trying to appear calm, but his eyes betrayed anxiety. He did not even greet Ann, but began immediately, "Herr Weiss is here."

153

"Herr Weiss?" Ann repeated. "The girls' father?"

"Yes, yes," the doctor spoke rapidly. "He was let out of the concentration camp yesterday. He went first to his house and found the doors sealed, but by that time the demonstrations had started, so he decided it would be better not to attract attention. He found a back alley and sat there till morning. He did not want to go to any friend's house for fear of causing them harm. Then he remembered that I knew his wife, and thought that a hospital being a public place, he was not likely to get me into trouble by coming here. He is in your uncle's room."

Feeling slightly dazed, Ann followed the doctor. At her entrance, the man who was sitting rather awkwardly on the straightbacked visitor's chair in Uncle Dick's room stood up and bowed to her.

The first thing Ann noticed about him was his strong resemblance to Ilse, accentuated by the deadly pallor of his thin face. Ilse's eyes looked at her in the same sad and wondering way. He said in fairly good English, "Miss Lindsay, how can I thank you enough for so befriending my girls?"

Uncle Dick must have noticed Ann's blush for he cut the thanks short. "This is the story in a nutshell," he told Ann. "Herr Weiss was informed by the camp authorities that he was free but that he must leave Germany within ten days. They even drove him to Frankfurt in the camp truck. But he is afraid they intend to use him as a decoy, so he does not dare to contact his wife or his daughters."

"Oh, couldn't you come to Mylius Strasse *somehow?*" Ann exclaimed. "It would help Ilse so much!"

Herr Weiss who had covered his eyes with his hand, looked up. "You cannot imagine how I long to see them," he said. "All these months I had no idea what had become of my children. But I could bring danger to them, and to Frau Meixner too. Have you seen the morning papers? Thousands of Jews were arrested last night! I cannot understand why I was suddenly set free."

"The papers also say that all the Jews who have visas to go abroad will be freed," Uncle Dick reminded him. "You do have a visa, I understand."

Herr Weiss nodded. "Yes, I do, both for England and Switzerland, but my passport was left behind in the house together with my daughters' passports. I made sure they had separate ones just in case my wife and myself were detained."

"But the passports have been retrieved!" Ann broke in eagerly. She began to tell the whole story, then stopped, uncertain, and looked from Uncle Dick to the doctor. "Er . . . does Herr Weiss know about Rachel?"

The white-faced man sighed. "Yes. Doctor Fromm told me. But it may not be permanent. A spontaneous recovery often occurs in such cases."

A young nurse brought in a pile of newspapers for Uncle Dick, and Ann glanced at the headlines. They were all the same. *The German population has expressed its wrath against the Jewish assassins by demonstrating in practically every town.* She shuddered.

They sat and talked for another hour. It was Uncle Dick who finally closed the discussion. "So it's all settled then," he said. "Ann is to call Frau Oberin and tell her Herr Weiss is here. She must know as soon as possible because it will undoubtedly affect whatever plans she may be making for Doctor Weiss and the girls. Doctor Fromm will break the news to Ilse and to Frau Meixner. Now, what about lodgings for Herr Weiss? He can't spend every night in back alleys."

155

"I have made arrangements," Doctor Fromm said, looking pleased. "An orderly has agreed to take Herr Weiss in. He has been employed here for many years and is thoroughly trustworthy."

"Good," said Uncle Dick. "As for the nurses, I have already told them that Herr Weiss is a business associate who has brought papers for me to sign. That should do it."

Ann started for home feeling a little uneasy. She knew it would be difficult to avoid Frau Meixner's questions as to why Uncle Dick wanted to see her so urgently. But, quite unexpectedly, Frau Meixner herself solved the problem. She met Ann at the door, dressed in her best black cloth coat, a small hat of lilac velvet perched on top of her red hair, and a worried expression on her face. Peter's teacher had telephoned again, she explained to Ann. It seemed that Peter was constantly getting into fights with his classmates and had very nearly broken someone's nose. "Now the principal wants to see me to discuss his behavior." Frau Meixner smoothed her gloves nervously. "But what can I tell him? How can I explain the situation? Oh dear, oh dear!" She went at last, leaving Ann standing in the middle of the hall.

Ann's first thought was that she must telephone now, before Frau Meixner came back and while Peter was still at school. She threw off her coat and hurried into the parlor. The receiver already in her hand, she paused. There must be no more running headlong into things as she had the first time. "Avoid using names," Uncle Dick had cautioned. Well, that was the first point. Second, she must compose a message that would convey briefly but clearly what she had to tell Frau Oberin. Ann thought for a minute then gave the number to the operator.

This time an elderly voice answered. "St. Gertrude's convent."

Holding the receiver tight, Ann said, "May I speak to Frau Oberin, please," and without waiting for an answer went on, "I met her at the Domkirche a few days ago."

Nothing. Just silence. Then some faint whispers, a click, another click, and at last Frau Oberin's brisk, *"Guten Tag."*

Ann braced herself. She spoke in a low voice but very distinctly. "Their father is back."

If Frau Oberin gave a gasp, Ann did not hear it. The nun did not ask any questions, but simply gave an order; "Stay at home this afternoon." That was all. The line went dead.

Is someone coming here this afternoon? Or will there be a letter? Or what? Ann was trying to guess as she slowly mounted the stairs. Absorbed in her thoughts, she opened the door of her room and was amazed to see Rachel sitting by the windowsill.

The little girl had never done anything like this before. Usually she spent all her time playing quietly by her sister's bed, although for the last few days, she had not even played, but had sat on the rug with one arm around Morritz and the other clutching the old clown on her lap. But now she was gurgling softly and pressing her face to the windowpane. Curious, Ann approached and peered over her shoulder.

In the street below, a small boy had got his legs entangled in the lead of a St. Bernard puppy. He was holding on to a lamppost and kicking to get free, but the puppy kept pulling in the opposite direction and binding his master tighter and tighter.

The scene apparently delighted Rachel. She went on

gurgling happily and pointing it out to Morritz, who was standing beside her on his hind legs.

Ann almost laughed too, but it suddenly struck her that the child could be seen from below. With a panicky, "No, no, darling. You mustn't," she seized the little girl by the waist and lowered her onto the floor.

She expected an uproar, but Rachel only gave her a long, wistful look and began to cry silently, her face in Morritz's fur. Ann felt like crying herself. It seemed so unfair that the child could not look out of the window, laugh at something funny, run along the tree-lined street. Dropping down on her knees, Ann hugged Rachel. "Everything is going to be all right, darling," she promised, and jumped up as the front doorbell began to ring. With a hasty, "Stay here quietly now," she raced downstairs.

It was only Frau Meixner, who had forgotten her key. She looked worn out and tearful. Her interview with Peter's headmaster had been brief. He had simply told her that if Peter continued to beat up his schoolmates, he would be expelled.

"He would not listen to me," Frau Meixner complained to Ann. "I told him the boy was often provoked, but he only shrugged his shoulders. He looked at me in a peculiar way, too, as if he knew about the Gestapo business. *Ah, mein Got!* I have such a headache. There are sandwiches and fruit for you and the girls, Fraulein Anna. I don't want any lunch."

Ann was sorry for Frau Meixner, but she could not help thinking that the headache was rather providential. By two in the afternoon the coast was clear for whatever Frau Oberin intended, and somehow Ann became more and more certain it would be a messenger. Frau Meixner was in her room, a towel soaked in vinegar tied over her head. The two girls were resting. Peter appeared briefly, snatched a sandwich, and disappeared again.

Ann installed herself at the kitchen table and tried to read, but she kept glancing at the clock. Two-thirty and still nothing happened. At a quarter to three the bell gave a faint ring. Ann ran into the hall, and unlocked the door.

A nun was standing on the steps, a flat book in mottled covers under one arm. She said in a clear voice that must have carried to the few people who passed by, "We are collecting for a Christmas dinner for our poor. Would you care to make a donation?"

It's the one I've seen outside Eleonore's house, Ann thought. She stepped back and said politely, *"Bitte kommen Sie herein."* They had just entered the parlor when Frau Meixner's sleepy voice called from upstairs, "Fraulein Anna, *wer ist da?"*

"Someone collecting for charity," Ann called back.

The nun lowered herself into the nearest armchair and placed her book on a small table. Her long hands with tapered fingers rested quietly in her lap. She bowed her head as if in prayer, and seemed to be silently gathering strength. Ann waited, tensely.

At last the nun took a deep breath and raised her head. Her big black eyes were full of weariness and sorrow. Her voice was soft, but her tone businesslike. "Frau Oberin sent me," she said, "because she considers it is safer than talking on the telephone. I am to tell you about the arrangements made to save Doctor Weiss's family." Her English was perfect, almost without accent. "Do not write anything down. Do your best to remember everything so you can repeat it to Herr Weiss."

159

"Will there be any long German names of people or places?" Ann asked anxiously.

The nun's lips moved as if she tried to smile but couldn't. "Very few," she said. "Frau Oberin's plans are always as simple and straightforward as Frau Oberin herself. She has told you, I think, that there is a branch of our convent near Basel. Her first intention was to provide the girls with false Aryan passports and get one of the nuns to drive them to Basel, pretending they were pupils from our orphanage who were being sent to convalesce in the mountain air. Now that Herr Weiss is back, though, the situation has changed. Also, the man who promised the passports now refuses. He has even returned the money Frau Oberin paid him to get an Aryan passport for Doctor Weiss. He is afraid. The times are too dangerous."

"He's right," Ann agreed, thinking of the newspaper headlines.

"Tell me," the nun went on, "how do you know Herr Weiss is back? Have you seen him?"

"This morning." Ann told briefly about her visit to the hospital and ended with, "He is afraid to come here. He thinks he might have been set free only to lead the Gestapo to his wife, and to his daughters, too."

"It could be true," the nun said thoughtfully. "On the other hand, his release from concentration camp might mean they have decided that Doctor Weiss has already left the country, in which case they would not be interested in the girls or their father any more. You told Frau Oberin that Herr Weiss and the girls all have their original passports and visas. Is that true?"

Ann nodded.

"Good," the nun said. "Then Frau Oberin's plan

should work." She began to speak rapidly in a low voice. "One of our sisters has a brother-in-law who owns a small hotel in Sandplacken, in the Taunus mountains—about half an hour by bus from Frankfurt. He intends to have the hotel redecorated and some repairs done before the ski season begins. So he will close down on November the fifteenth, that is next Tuesday, but the workmen won't be coming till Thursday, which means the place will be empty on Wednesday the sixteenth. Please memorize the date and the place."

"I won't forget," Ann promised, wondering why the date sounded familiar to her.

"Very well. Herr Weiss is to go to Sandplacken early on Wednesday morning. The door will be left unlocked. The girls are to join their father there at some time during the mid-morning."

"Frau Oberin wants them to hide in that hotel!" Ann exclaimed.

The nun stopped her with a gesture. "Wait. Let me explain. The man—and we will call him simply 'the hotel owner'—is willing to let Herr Weiss use his car to drive to Switzerland. He has friends in Basel and is sure there will be no trouble in getting the car back. But in case something happens, though we hope it won't, he will say the car was stolen from the garage. One more important thing; before starting for Sandplacken, Herr Weiss is to make plane reservations for three people, either to Geneva or London, it does not really matter. The object is to make the Gestapo concentrate their attention on the airport, if they *are* still interested in Heir Weiss."

"But the girls. . . . How are they going to get to Sandplacken without being seen?" Ann faltered. "In *daytime?*"

This time the nun really smiled. "Yes," she answered. "I agree there is a risk, but Frau Oberin is very insistent. In her opinion it will attract much less attention if they just walk out of the house sometime after nine, when most people have already gone to work and housewives are busy washing up breakfast dishes, than if they try creeping out at night. Besides, buses to the Taunus area do not run during the night. Even if people do notice the girls, they will probably merely think Frau Meixner has had guests staying in the house."

"And are they to travel alone?" Ann asked, still doubtful. "Ilse is very weak."

"She has five days in which to recuperate," the nun pointed out. "The news about her father, and that they are going away will help, too. Does she know yet about Herr Weiss? The doctor is going to tell her, I hope. You will see how it will cheer her."

The nun rose and moved toward the door. "Are you sure you will remember all the instructions?" she asked.

"Yes, I'm sure. But what about Doctor Weiss herself? Isn't she coming too? Ilse . . . she wonders if her mother still loves them."

"Tell Ilse never to have such doubts," the nun answered gravely. "Doctor Weiss sends her daughters her love. She wants them to know she is thinking of them constantly and is convinced that one day they will all be together again. As to her coming too, how could she? It is not possible for *her* to use the passport with her own name on it. She would be arrested immediately. No, we must wait until we can get an Aryan passport for her. We will manage it somehow."

Ann could hear Frau Meixner moving about upstairs and hoped her visitor would leave. But the nun remained standing. She asked abruptly, "You are friends with Eleonore Von Waldenfels, are you not?"

Ann, who was trying to decide whether Frau Meixner was coming down the stairs, said, "Yes, we are friends. Why? Do you know her?"

"I knew her mother. Does she ever speak about her? I thought with a girl of her own age she might talk more openly than . . . let us say with her father."

Ann shifted from foot to foot. "Well, I—"

"Does she feel bitter about her mother leaving the family?"

Ann almost wished Frau Meixner would appear. She stammered unhappily, "Yes, she does."

"I see. Well, goodbye, my dear. Call Frau Oberin if you really must, but do be careful."

"Goodbye . . ." Ann hesitated, realizing she did not know the nun's name.

"Sister Josefa." The nun picked up her book and left, moving softly in her heavy shoes.

17

Peter in Trouble

Uncle Dick whistled softly when he heard Frau Oberin's scheme. "But actually her idea makes sense," he admitted. "It probably will work and it's certainly easier for the girls than trying a more complicated maneuver. You do think that Ilse is better?"

"Much better," Ann assured him. "This morning she asked Frau Meixner to help her to dress and she ate a good breakfast."

Doctor Fromm, who was pacing the room, muttered, "Nervous energy. She might collapse again at any moment." He shook his head doubtfully. "I am anxious," he said. "The girls to walk out of the house openly . . . take a bus . . ."

"Perhaps I could drive them," Uncle Dick suggested.

"I feel well enough and the car is repaired. All I have to do is phone the garage."

Doctor Fromm raised his hands. "Herr Lindsay! You must not get behind the wheel for at least a month *after* you are out of the hospital. No, no, let's accept Frau Oberin's decision. I will explain the situation to Herr Weiss this evening and then to Frau Meixner. I only hope she will be sensible and will not go into hysterics when she hears about it."

Surprisingly, Frau Meixner did not go into hysterics. She was insistent only on one point: the girls were not to travel to Sandplacken alone. She would go with them. "Those poor children," she declared. "Ilse is not fit yet to go alone, *and* look after her sister and the dog as well."

"So Doctor Fromm simply had to agree," Ann told Uncle Dick the next day. "But he persuaded Frau Meixner not to leave the house with the girls. She is to join them a little later at the streetcar stop."

"Streetcar? I thought they were going by bus."

"You have to take the streetcar first and then change to a bus."

"I see. Well, now let's talk about another matter. Do the two girls have any decent clothes for traveling?"

Ann thought for a moment. "Frau Meixner made a skirt for each of them," she explained, "and she knitted twin sets to match the skirts. They make rather nice outfits. The skirts are gray and the twin sets have tiny red . . ."

Uncle Dick waved his hand. "All right, all right. Never mind the fashion details. What about coats? It's quite cold and it seems to rain almost every day."

"They only have their old raincoats—the ones they had on when the Gestapo came to their house."

165

"Then get them new ones." Uncle Dick took a wallet out of his bedside-table drawer and handed Ann a few banknotes.

"Oh, thank you ever so much, Uncle Dick," Ann breathed fervently, "but can you afford it? Remember what you said about the hospital bills?"

He laughed. "Don't worry. I'm not giving our last pennies away. The articles I sent to London a couple of weeks ago will take care of the bills. The chief was probably cursing because they were handwritten, but I explained in my letter that my typewriter was smashed beyond repair."

"Ilse will be delighted," Ann said excitedly, putting the money in her handbag. "And Rachel too."

"I hope their father won't take it as an act of charity," Uncle Dick said, frowning. "He has considerable amounts of money deposited in Geneva and London. Money in the bank is a must for Jews who apply for visas. But right now all he has are the clothes on his back. Never mind. Just buy the coats."

As it turned out, Ann spent the rest of the week shopping. The girls needed new underwear, stockings, shoes. Doctor Fromm produced some money, saying that Herr Weiss would reimburse him later, and Ann gladly ran around the shops. The saleslady in the shoe shop looked a little surprised that Ann's "sisters" would not come to be fitted, but Ann mumbled something about their being sick, and blushed scarlet.

But that was the only snag. The rest of the shopping went smoothly. Ann was especially pleased with the coats which were just right for the season—warm but not too thick or heavy. The pattern of small checks in two tones of blue was very attractive and Uncle Dick was so pleased when she showed him her purchases that he ordered her to go back to the same shop and buy one for herself. "Get a green one. You'll look good in it," he advised and Ann was only too glad to oblige.

There was a dress rehearsal on Sunday and that was when Ann discovered that the two Jewish girls had no hats. The supply of money she kept in a separate envelope in her bag was very low. Well, she could buy them warm berets on Monday. Lots of people in the street were wearing berets and they were cheap.

It was not easy to find berets to match the coats, but Ann found a small shop that had berets of almost every color. She even bought one for herself with her own money.

Pleased with her shopping spree and feeling very hungry, Ann got out of the streetcar and turned toward Mylius Strasse. It was almost twelve. She was just in time for lunch. Peter would not be at home because the whole class was going to visit the Kronberg castle, which was not far from Frankfurt. "We are going in a chartered bus," Peter explained grandly. "That means only *we* can ride in it, and everybody is to bring a lunch box."

Maybe, Ann thought recklessly, as she approached the house, the girls could come downstairs for lunch. To celebrate their last day but one in Mylius Strasse.

Dashing up the front steps, she unlocked the door and stepped inside. A strong smell of disinfectant mixed with the acrid odor of burning greeted her. The kitchen was deserted, but a pot was sizzling and smoking on the stove. Ann turned off the gas, threw her parcels onto the nearest chair and hurried upstairs. She had just reached the landing when Frau Meixner came out of Peter's room with a crumpled towel in her hands.

One look at the older woman's face and Ann realized that something terrible had happened. "The girls?" she gasped, then saw through the opened door Peter lying in bed, a bandage on his head.

"Oh, Fraulein Anna!" Frau Meixner cried, kneading the towel and wiping her eyes with it. "Just think! Peter's classmates did not want him to go on the outing with them. They would not let him on the bus and when he still tried to get on, they beat him up. The teacher in charge intervened, but it was too late. They had already beaten Peter viciously!"

From his bed, Peter called, "The teacher hardly intervened at all."

"Don't talk! Rest," Frau Meixner ordered. "I called Doctor Fromm at the hospital," she told Ann. "He said Peter must be kept very quiet. He will examine him as soon as he has finished his rounds. Oh, Fraulein Anna, just look! Isn't it terrible?"

Ann came closer. Peter was certainly a sad sight. Blood trickled from under the gauze bandage on his forehead, his left eye was almost closed and the thin arms sticking out of the short sleeves of his pajamas were marbled blue and black.

"Don't stare at me," Peter growled. "I am not hurt that much and I want something to eat. I mean *real* food, not that stuff!" He pushed away the tray with a bowl of gruel which was standing on a chair beside his bed. "There is nothing wrong with my insides."

"Let me bring him some of our lunch," Ann offered and escaped before Frau Meixner could stop her.

It occurred to her, as she entered the kitchen, that the whole lunch might have been ruined, leaving nothing to take to Peter, but closer inspection showed that the damage was not as bad as that. Boiled beef was cooking peacefully in its pot and the baked apples in the oven were just done. Only the potatoes were burned into a sticky black mass.

Ann took a small portion of the beef and a baked apple to Peter, then quickly returned to the kitchen. Knowing how Frau Meixner treasured every pot and pan, she wanted to scrape out the potato pot before the mess inside hardened. It looked a hopeless task, but she had heard or read somewhere that burned pots could be cleaned by boiling baking soda in them. Well, it was worth a try.

Ann rummaged on the shelves until she found a can of baking soda. It had a picture of a birthday cake on it. *A birthday cake!* Ann stared at it with a sinking heart. She had forgotten all about Eleonore's birthday! November the sixteenth. Tomorrow. . . . No, *Wednesday,* the day the girls were to leave! Ann thought quickly. She could still go, of course—Eleonore was not expecting her until eleven. But what about Peter? Could Frau Meixner leave him? Two days . . . surely he would be well enough by Wednesday. With this comforting thought, Ann poured a generous portion of soda into the pot.

Doctor Fromm came in the afternoon and seemed less optimistic. He did say that Peter was in pretty good shape considering the beating he had received, but warned of something called "the latent effect of shock," and advised Frau Meixner to keep Peter warm and quiet.

On Tuesday morning Peter was still all right. Ann and Ilse took turns sitting with him and trying to amuse him. But by early afternoon he was running a slight temperature, and by the evening he was burning.

"Just when the doctor is on night duty," Frau Meixner lamented. "Oh, Fraulein Anna, what is going to happen tomorrow morning?"

Ann already knew what was going to happen. "I'll go with the girls," she said, trying to sound very matter-of-fact about it. "There's nothing to it, really, Frau Meixner. I'll just leave the girls with their father and take the bus back."

Frau Meixner shook her head. "I don't know, Fraulein Anna. You make it sound so easy, but I have my doubts about the whole scheme. What would your Herr uncle say if something should happen to you?"

Ann knew only too well what Uncle Dick would say. He thought she was too deeply involved already. So she answered quickly, "I don't want to make him anxious. I'll tell him afterward. Don't worry, nothing will happen to me."

"They *could* go alone, but I don't know if Ilse could manage . . ." Frau Meixner's voice faltered.

Ann thought for a moment. It wasn't anything very difficult: just to take the streetcar to the last stop, get out and take the bus to Sandplacken. But Ilse was bound to be nervous, drop her change, or lose their tickets. She might talk to Rachel even though the child could not answer, and that would attract attention. Ever since Ilse had heard of her father's release, she had talked constantly—about how they were going to emigrate to the United States, how some famous doctor would cure Rachel, how her father would buy a house in California with a big garden. . . . She talked on and on and sometimes the talking ended in sobs.

"All this will disappear as soon as she is in normal conditions," the doctor had said. But in the meantime . . .

No, Ann decided, Ilse could not be trusted to go alone with Rachel. Frau Meixner was apparently thinking the same because she did not raise any further objections, but only advised Ann to go to bed early and get a good night's rest.

"Oh, I will," Ann promised. "But it's only a quarter to eight and I want to run over to the doctor's house and ask Minna to do something for me tomorrow."

Going to her room, she hastily wrote a note to Eleonore, explaining that she could not come to the birthday party. *My uncle has made arrangements that make it impossible,* was the best she could do. The idea of talking to Eleonore on the telephone made her shudder. Before she knew it, Eleonore would make her tell about the trip to Sandplacken and everything. Writing was much easier, and she would ask Minna to deliver the note in the morning, so that even if Eleonore did call, she would not be there.

Having finished the note, Ann opened the top drawer of her dresser and took out a square package wrapped in white tissue paper and tied with a green ribbon. She had bought *The Legends of Ireland* in a big bookshop in Kaiser Strasse that stocked foreign books. Eleonore had once mentioned she wanted to read this book and it was beautifully illustrated. Ann had spent all her weekly allowance on it.

The package under her arm, Ann rang the bell of Doctor Fromm's house. Minna took a long time opening the door and Ann was afraid she might have already gone to bed. But Minna appeared at last, clad in a blue bathrobe, and Ann was solemnly conducted into the parlor.

She explained what she wanted to Minna, trying to make it as simple as possible. "But please do not go before ten o'clock," she urged. *"Ten.* You do understand, don't you?" She pointed at the grandfather clock.

Minna nodded gravely. "Yes. When the big hand is on the twelve and the small on the ten."

"That's right," Ann said. "Please don't forget."

Minna gave her a wide-eyed look. "I won't forget. Tomorrow is a special day."

"Special day?" Ann asked, puzzled. "Why? Is it your birthday too?"

Minna looked shocked, "Oh, *nein!*" She folded her hands and recited as if she were in class, "It-is-the-day-we-celebrate - the - memory - of - our - venerated - patron St. Gertrude."

"Oh, I see!" Ann exclaimed. "St. Gertrude. . . . I suppose you had a big celebration at the convent."

"It was a beautiful day," Minna said with deep conviction. "In the morning we had chocolate instead of milk and we had no lessons. We went to solemn Mass and then we played. And the sisters played with us. Sister Ludowina could skip better than any of us. Then we had a marvelous dinner and a special cake for dessert. It had yellow cream inside and pink sugar on top. It was so good!"

"Perhaps you could bake a cake like that yourself," Ann suggested, amused and at the same time touched by these reminiscences.

"Nein," Minna said sadly. "I couldn't. Sister Brunhilda never let anyone enter the kitchen when she was baking that cake. She said the cream would curdle if people breathed on it."

She pouted and looked down, fingering the cord of her bathrobe. "I *always* went to the convent for the celebration," she said. "But this year Frau Oberin did not invite me. Why?"

"Maybe they're not having a celebration this year," Ann said, trying to invent a good reason, but realizing quite well why the Mother Superior did not want any strangers in the convent. "Everything is so expensive," she suggested at last. "Maybe they can't afford the cake this year."

"Maybe," Minna said softly, but she did not sound convinced and her "Goodbye, Fraulein Anna," sounded wistful and sad.

Before going to bed, Ann decided to look at Peter. He was lying on his back and staring at the ceiling. When Ann came in, he turned on his side and asked, "Is she going to take the dog with her?"

Ann understood. "Morritz belongs to Rachel, Peter," she told him gently. "You couldn't ask her to leave him behind. He's her only friend. They sit together for hours and 'talk' to each other."

Peter turned his face to the wall. "She has him. I have no friends at all."

Ann wanted badly to say something sympathetic, but she was afraid of upsetting the boy even more. So she only murmured, *"Gute Nacht,* Peter," and left the room.

18

The Sandplacken Inn

Ann had expected the next morning to be a hectic one, but everything went with an almost uncanny smoothness. Frau Meixner looked very tired because Peter had been restless during the night and she had sat up with him. But she managed to get up early and prepare breakfast. She was still uneasy about Ann going to Sandplacken and at the last minute she called the doctor at home. Minna answered and told her that her brother was still at the hospital.

"I suppose you will have to go, Fraulein Anna, but I don't like it," Frau Meixner said repeatedly as she buttoned Rachel into her new coat.

At about twenty minutes to ten the three girls left the house. Rachel had Morritz on a lead. They waved to

Frau Meixner standing on the steps and went toward Gruneburg Weg, Ann talking loudly in English. It had been decided that should any of the neighbors ask questions, Frau Meixner would say that Ann had two cousins staying overnight, and that she was going to the station to see them off.

As they passed the doctor's house, Ann thought she saw the curtain in one window rise slightly, but she was not sure. She hoped Minna was not watching. Never mind, she told herself, if Minna said anything to Eleonore, she would just stick to the story of her cousins passing through Frankfurt and visiting her. Would Eleonore believe it? Would anyone believe it? It did not matter really, because by that time the girls and their father would be far away.

A few more steps and Mylius Strasse was left behind. Ann tried to walk casually, but every time a passerby gave them a glance her heart sank. Did the three of them look like ordinary girls in trim new coats, or would people notice that Ilse was abnormally pale—that she, Ann, was clasping Rachel's hand too tightly, and that Rachel herself was staring around as if she had never seen a street before?

But no one stopped them, no one said anything until they got off the streetcar and were in the bus. Then a woman drew up her feet at the sight of Morritz and said that it was a disgrace that dogs were allowed in buses.

The bus moved quickly because there were only a few passengers at each of the stops. Soon they were out of the city and greenery began to flash past the windows. A few more sharp turns of the road, and pines could be seen climbing the mountain slopes. The foggy day was slowly brightening as pale sunlight pierced the gray mist. "Sandplacken," the driver announced, and the three girls tumbled off the bus.

When the bus was out of sight, Ilse asked in a whisper, "Which way?"

"Across the road and to the right," Ann answered also in a whisper, but then decided that it was ridiculous and went on in her ordinary voice, "It's just a few minutes' walk. Come on."

Keeping tightly together, they crossed the road and turned into a much narrower one, bordered by pine-woods, Morritz tugging at the lead and sniffing eagerly at the underbrush.

The inn came in sight sooner than Ann expected—a low, white frame house with an open porch on three sides. The girls stopped as if by command. Rachel's eyes traveled questioningly from the house to her sister's face and back again. A slight wind rippled the pine branches. The sun, so bright only a minute ago, now hid behind a cloud, and a bird cried sharply somewhere high up in a tree. A sudden feeling of panic seized Ann. She wanted to cry out, "Let's go back!" but realized it was absurd. It was too late anyway, because Herr Weiss appeared from around the house.

Ilse gasped, "Papa!" and ran forward, but it was Rachel who reached him first. Herr Weiss lifted her onto his shoulder, and, keeping one arm tightly around her, held out the other one to Ilse.

Ann picked up Morritz's lead, which Rachel had dropped, and walked slowly across the yard, anxious not to interfere with the girls' first meeting with their father. But Herr Weiss would not linger outside. With a quick, "Don't stand here," he led his daughters to the side door and beckoned to Ann to follow them.

Inside, a short hall led into a big, whitewashed kitchen with an enormous gas stove in the middle and copper pans on the wall. Putting Rachel down, Herr Weiss squatted in front of her and kissed her several times, saying, "Everything will be all right now, darling. We will make it all right."

Ilse was holding on to her father's shoulder and rubbing her face against his hair. "It is only now that I really believe it," she said in a choked voice. "I am . . ." She broke off and raised her hand. "Listen!" she whispered.

Tires swished underneath the window. Herr Weiss sprang to his feet and pushing the three girls behind the kitchen table, stood in front of it. The back door opened. Morritz began to growl. Instinctively, Ann shortened his lead.

A man in a long black raincoat appeared on the threshold. Ann recognized him immediately. It was Gunter, the man who had searched Frau Meixner's attic. Only this time, *he* was in command—the man looming behind his shoulder was obviously a subordinate and probably a new member of the Gestapo forces. He was young and round-faced and cringed every time Gunter glanced in his direction.

Gunter's cold eyes swept the room, checking every person in it. When he looked at Ann, she tried to return his gaze with a defiant glare, but something inside her was already numb with fear.

Still without saying a word, Gunter looked around again. He frowned and it seemed to Ann that an expression of disappointment crossed his face. It took her a moment to realize the reason. Of course! He expected to find Doctor Weiss!

Scowling, Gunter took a step toward the little group by

the kitchen table. "All right, Weiss," he said roughly. "No more of your games. Where is your wife?"

Herr Weiss answered calmly, "I am sure she is already abroad. My daughters and I are leaving too. We have our plane tickets."

"Good." Gunter's tone changed. Now it was smooth, almost friendly. "And you can use your plane tickets as soon as we have had a talk with your wife. Come, man! She is supposed to join you here? Right? Well, we just want to ask her a few simple questions and then she can leave with you. We don't want you Jews. The sooner this country is rid of you, the better."

Herr Weiss raised his head. "I have told you already. I do not know where my wife is."

Gunter shouted, "You Jewish swine! Don't you know you may not look an Aryan in the eyes!" His fist swung out and Herr Weiss sagged under the blow. Ilse gave a stifled scream and tried to reach out for her father, but he stopped her with a gesture. Rachel stood motionless. She did not utter a sound, but Ann winced as she saw the terror in the child's eyes.

Then suddenly, something quite unexpected happened. The telephone hanging on the wall began to ring. Gunter reached it in one long stride and took off the receiver. Clutching at the lead so that it almost became embedded in her palm, Ann trembled. The call could be from Uncle Dick, Frau Oberin—any of them. The inn was in the telephone book: it would be easy enough to find the number.

But Gunter's reaction made it clear that the call must be from Gestapo quarters. "What?" he said with amazement. "*What* did you say? You have found her?" He pressed the receiver tighter against his ear. "Where? I can't hear you. In St. Gertrude's convent? When? I see."

Ann kept her eyes fixed on a spot between Morritz's ears. She could not bear to look at Ilse or her father, but she saw the crumpled, bloodstained handkerchief Herr Weiss had been pressing to his face, flutter to the ground, and heard Ilse's heavy breathing.

Gunter went on talking. *"Nein!"* he shouted defensively into the telephone. "We had no leads at all in that direction. How did the informant know? Oh, an *anonymous* call! Did it sound like a man or a woman? Come, come, that is not likely! You are imagining it. Speak louder. No, that would hardly be necessary. Just make it clear to her that her husband and *children*," he stressed the word, "are under arrest and that she had better talk if she wants them to remain unharmed. Right. In about half an hour."

Gunter hung up and turned to Ann. *"Heraus!"* he ordered.

As she did not move immediately, he repeated impatiently, "I said *out*," and she knew she had to go. For the first time since that fateful telephone message she dared to look at the girls and their father. He stood with his head bent, his face swollen. Ilse's white face merged with the wall behind her. Rachel clung to her sister with both hands. It was dreadful to leave them, but Gunter was holding the door open and Ann knew she must go. She was almost by the door when she realized she still had Morritz with her. As she stopped, not knowing what to do because Ilse seemed in a state of stupor and Rachel was now crying uncontrollably, Gunter came over and, taking the lead from her, tied Morritz to the table. "Good dog," he said, fondling Morritz's ears.

Ann went out. Behind her, Gunter was giving orders

to his subordinate. "Keep an eye on them. I will tele-phone further instructions."

A sleek gray sedan stood in front of the door. Gunter slid into the driver's seat and motioned to Ann to sit be-side him. The car moved off. Ann turned her face toward the window and tried to look calm, but it was difficult. Where was Gunter taking her? Was she under arrest? Would the Gestapo arrest Uncle Dick too?

She received the answer to all her questions at the same time. Gunter stopped the car a block away from Grune-burg Weg and opened the door. "If you were not a child, Miss Lindsay," he said, stressing every word, "we would have treated this matter very differently. I hope you are conscious of this fact. We cannot prove anything against your uncle since he is in the hospital and to our knowledge has never left it all this time. However, please inform him that we would like both of you to leave Ger-many before the end of this week. You may go."

Ann jumped onto the pavement. She stood watching the car move away, feeling a little dizzy. But it did not last long. She was free after all, and surely she could still do something to help. But to whom should she turn? Frau Meixner? The doctor? Frau Oberin? No, all three were in danger themselves. Frau Oberin might already have been arrested for harboring a Jew in the convent. *The informant,* Gunter had said. Who could it be? She supposed it might have been someone who had stumbled accidentally on proof that Doctor Weiss was being hidden by the nuns. Anyway, that was not important at the mo-ment. The important thing now was to get help. . . .

Ann walked on rapidly, trying to think of something she could do and, being so absorbed, she bumped straight into a young officer who stepped back and almost fell off the pavement. She did not even stop to apologize, but raced down the street as fast as her feet could carry her. The sight of the military uniform had reminded her of the one person who might be able to help: Colonel Von Waldenfels. He seemed kind and he adored his daughter. Maybe he would do something, if not for Doctor Weiss or her husband, then for the girls. After all, Ilse was Eleonore's age. . . . It was worth trying anyhow. She quickened her steps even more.

Through the door of the block of flats . . . across the lobby and into the elevator. "Is Colonel Von Waldenfels at home?" Ann asked breathlessly when Trudi opened the door.

The maid did not look as perky as usual. She seemed tired and her apron was askew. "Fraulein Lindsay . . ." she faltered. "We were not expecting you. You said you were not coming. The colonel is at home, but he is resting. And," Trudi glanced over her shoulder, lowering her voice, "he is quite upset because of the scene Fraulein Eleonore made when she received your message."

"A scene because I could not come?" Ann asked, sincerely surprised. "I am sorry, I really couldn't. But *please* ask the colonel if I may speak to him. It is very important."

"Yes, Fraulein." Trudi disappeared and Ann went toward Eleonore's room. There seemed to be no harm in seeing her for a minute and saying how sorry she was she had to miss the party.

Eleonore was curled up in her chair. At the sight of Ann she sat up and flushed angrily. "So, you decided to come after all?" she said. "You needn't have bothered. It is all over."

"What's over?" Ann asked, straining her ears for the

sound of the colonel's footsteps.

"My party, that's what!" Eleonore's voice rose stridently then sank into a long sob. "I had planned it so carefully. Papa ordered a special dessert from a restaurant and in the afternoon a man was to come with a puppet theatre. Not some silly children's show, but a real play. I made Papa cancel everything."

"I couldn't help it," Ann said, looking with pity at Eleonore's swollen eyes. "Did you get my present? I asked Minna to give it to you with my note."

"I got it all right and that miserable dwarf brought me a gift too, a hideous orange purse she said she crocheted herself. She and I had a long talk."

There was something threatening in Eleonore's tone, but Ann was too tense to play guessing games. "Look," she said sharply. "If you have something to tell me, do so. I have very little time."

"Oh, all right. I *will* tell you and it won't take long." Eleonore was openly gloating now. "You see, I could not quite believe that you would give up my party without having a pretty good reason and since you did not bother to explain anything in your note, I decided to find out from that Minna creature just what you were up to."

Ann did not answer. She was thinking desperately: But Minna does not know a thing. What could she have said?

Eleonore smiled triumphantly. "It was easy enough to make the halfwit talk. I promised her my Madame La Marquise and she told me the whole story."

Instinctively, Ann glanced toward the bookcase. The doll was gone.

Eleonore eyed her with interest. "Quite a shock to you, isn't it? You did not expect it, did you? Well, it so happened that Minna saw you this morning leaving the house with two other girls. You were all three dressed in your best clothes, she said. She also told me that November the sixteenth was St. Gertrude's day and that there was always a big celebration at St. Gertrude's convent. Minna was quite hurt that the Mother Superior had invited you and your friends but left her out. What that poor idiot did not realize was that those two girls were Jewish, the ones the Gestapo were searching for. Frau Meixner was hiding them in her house and you helped her, didn't you? Only neither of you were careful enough. Trudi saw a child sitting on the windowsill a few days ago, and twice I saw an older girl peering between the curtains. It was getting too dangerous for Frau Meixner to keep those girls, especially after the Gestapo had searched her house. Wasn't it? So she made arrangements with the convent to take over. She is a Catholic. Trudi saw her going to St. Ignatius church. So today you smuggled those Jewish girls into the convent among the other guests. You thought no one would notice and that you played safe, didn't you, but it did not work after all."

Eleonore stopped speaking, but as Ann only gave her a long, bewildered stare, she rushed on. "The minute that ugly idiot left, I telephoned the Gestapo and told them there were Jews hiding at St. Gertrude's convent."

"*What* did you say, Eleonore?"

Colonel Von Waldenfels appeared in the door, his face gray, the collar of his uniform open at the throat. "What did you say?" he repeated hoarsely.

Eleonore said peevishly, "You startled me, Papa. I only said that I told the Gestapo that there were Jews hiding at St. Gertrude's convent."

"You sent the Gestapo to St. Gertrude's? Do you realize what you have done?" The colonel strode over to the wheelchair and, taking Eleonore by the shoulders, made her face him. "Your *mother* is there," he said. "Suppose . . . they have found her. Oh, God." His voice broke, and he stood looking down at Eleonore as if he had met her for the first time.

Eleonore pouted. "Mama? She did not leave us to enter a convent. You know *that*, Papa."

"No, she did not leave us to enter a convent," the colonel said in a strange flat voice. "She left us to save my career and maybe my life. But mainly she left because of *you*. She hoped that as long as she was not here and because of my position, the fact that your mother was Jewish would be overlooked."

Eleonore paled. "It is not true!" she cried wildly. "Mama was Italian."

"There are Italian Jews too, Eleonore. Your mother did go back to Italy under her maiden name, and she never wrote because she thought it would be safer for me not to keep in touch with her. But a few months ago she happened to see in an old issue of a German newspaper a small notice about your accident. She wanted to know whether you had recovered, how you were getting on. But she knew she could not get a visa, so she crossed the border illegally. Somehow she made contact with one of the sisters at St. Gertrude's. They took her in as 'Sister Josefa'. I met her, talked to her . . ." His voice died away and he swallowed painfully before continuing in a low voice, "I knew who she was, the minute the porter described the nun who asked after you. I knew she was waiting, hoping to get some glimpse of you. I thought she was safe in the convent, and now . . ." His mouth suddenly quivered and he bent tenderly over Eleonore. "Don't look like that, darling," he said pityingly. "I was too abrupt. The Gestapo may not have found her after all."

Eleonore pushed her father's hand away. Tears were streaming down her face and she clutched at the arms of her chair, screaming. "A *Mischling!* I am a Mischling! Papa, say it's not true. *Please* say it!"

"My poor child," said the colonel. "You will have to get used to the idea sooner or later." Then looking at Ann as though noticing her for the first time, he said politely, "Trudi said you asked to see me."

In an agony of embarrassment, Ann mumbled something to the effect that it could wait. There was no use pleading with him now to save the girls. His own tragedy was too closely involved. She wanted only to get away. She averted her gaze from the sobbing, screaming figure in the wheelchair and fled from the room.

Just outside the door stood a big wastepaper basket with a broom and pail beside it. Trudi must have been sweeping up when she answered Ann's ring. The basket was full to overflowing with torn and crumpled party decorations and broken china. Ann recognized the remains of the gnome holding a stamp box which had stood on Eleonore's table. There was something else, too—*The Legends of Ireland,* its cover wrenched off and its pages torn across.

Ann hurried past the basket and across the hall. As she stepped into the elevator she thought how strange it was that she would probably never see Eleonore again.

It was cold and windy outside. She walked slowly, for now there seemed no point in hurrying. All she could do was go to Uncle Dick and tell him everything. She pulled her scarf up so that no one would see she was crying and made her way toward the streetcar stop and the hospital.

19

Sister Josefa

U<small>NCLE</small> D<small>ICK</small> was standing in the middle of the room, fully dressed. His topcoat lay across the foot of the bed. He did not seem surprised to see her, but his greeting was a curt, "The Mother Superior called about fifteen minutes ago."

Her mind still on Eleonore, Ann answered dully, "Did she? About Doctor Weiss being arrested. We can't help her, I'm afraid. No one can."

Uncle Dick frowned. "Wait a minute. Let's get things straight. I must admit I understood only part of what Frau Oberin was saying. She insisted on speaking in English and her accent is so thick I had to guess at most of it. But I think I got the general idea. The Gestapo came to the convent around ten this morning. They did not say

186

for whom or what they were looking, but they searched the convent and somehow found a document with Doctor Weiss's name on it. I think it must have been her doctor's diploma. She probably thought she would need it abroad in case she wanted to practice. Well, the Gestapo officer gave the Mother Superior an ultimatum: she was either to produce Doctor Weiss within the next few minutes, or all the sisters would be arrested and the convent closed for good."

Ann nodded. "And Doctor Weiss gave herself up."

Her uncle waved his hand impatiently. "Wait. Let me finish. Doctor Weiss *did* give herself up, but it was not the real Doctor Weiss. One of the nuns, a Sister Josefa, volunteered to go in her stead. She pretended she was Doctor Weiss, for it had become evident that none of the Gestapo men knew Doctor Weiss by sight. They could not tell the difference."

"Sister Josefa!" Ann exclaimed. "But that's Eleonore's mother."

"Eleonore Von Waldenfels? What do you mean?"

Ann told him about the day's happenings, hurrying over Eleonore's part. It was too painful to talk about it. While she spoke, Uncle Dick moved about the room, taking his things out of drawers and packing them into a suitcase that stood open on a chair. When she finished he said simply, "I see. Press down on that suitcase so that I can lock it, will you? You say the Gestapo has ordered us out of Germany within the week. Well, we can do better than that. We're leaving right now."

Ann looked up quickly. "Leaving? But what about the girls and Herr Weiss? If we go now we'll never know what's happened to them."

Uncle Dick's eyebrows rose. "Who says so? On the contrary, we're going to find out pretty soon. Yes, come in."

A nurse entered almost running. "Herr Lindsay! There is a man from the garage here. He says you asked for your car to be brought round. It is waiting in front of the building."

"That's right," Uncle Dick answered nonchalantly. "Thank you."

But the nurse would not be brushed off so casually. "Herr Lindsay, you cannot leave the hospital without being discharged! It is impossible."

Uncle Dick picked up the suitcase. "Just a short business trip. I'm afraid it cannot be avoided."

"But you are coming straight back? I can tell Herr Doctor Fromm?" the nurse insisted, eyeing the suitcase.

"Certainly. Come on, Ann."

They went rapidly down the corridor. In the lobby, Uncle Dick stopped, checked something quickly in the telephone book and wrote a number on his cuff. Outside it was beginning to rain and umbrellas were mushrooming along the pavements. A uniformed chauffeur was standing beside the familiar blue car. Uncle Dick paid him off and slid behind the wheel. "Get in," he told Ann. "What are you waiting for?"

Ann shrank back. Her drive with the Gestapo officer had been her first since the accident, but then she had been too frightened to care. Now, the mere idea of sitting down on those familiar red-cushioned seats made her feel sick. But, gritting her teeth, she edged in beside Uncle Dick.

"I thought you weren't supposed to drive," she managed to say as he started the engine and the car moved slowly forward.

"Can't be helped, can it," he said. "Do you know how

to get to the convent from here?"

"I don't know where it is at all," Ann said faintly.

She heard a rustle of paper. Uncle Dick was consulting the city map. When they started again, she realized they were heading for old Frankfurt. Rain began to drum on the car roof.

"Here we are," Uncle Dick said at last, and Ann forced herself to look up. The convent was smaller than she had imagined it. Built of stones darkened by age, it looked like the hull of a ship. The massive front door had a giant cross carved on it.

"Let's see if there is a back entrance. No sense in attracting attention." Uncle Dick nosed the car slowly down a narrow alley.

"I think someone has seen us," Ann murmured, craning her neck to look back. "I saw a face at one of those small windows beside the door."

The back wall of the convent came in sight. It had no windows at all, only a small oak door also carved with a cross. As they approached, this door opened a crack and an arm in a wide black sleeve appeared.

Uncle Dick maneuvered the car so that it stopped directly in front of the door. Frau Oberin came down the two stone steps leading to the pavement, followed closely by a young dark-haired woman in a black cloth coat.

"Herr Lindsay, thank God you have come," Frau Oberin said in German. "This is Doctor Weiss. Please help her." She seized the young woman by the elbow and pushed her toward the car.

"How can you ask me to leave like this, Reverend Mother?" said the young woman distractedly. "Sister Josefa! What will happen to her?"

"I am not asking you. I am ordering you to go," said

Frau Oberin. "There is nothing more you can do here. Your duty now is to your family."

Uncle Dick put his head out of the window. "Get inside, please," he said. "We are all risking our lives standing here."

Ann held the back door open and Doctor Weiss got in. Frau Oberin raised her hand, said quietly, *"Gott sei mit Ihnen,"* and the car sped off.

Doctor Weiss sat very still, looking in front of her. Glancing back, Ann could see that her face was softly oval like Rachel's and that she had the same curly hair, but there was a yellow tinge to her skin that spoke of long confinement indoors.

In and out, in and out of the narrow streets they went. Uncle Dick must have studied the map very carefully. However, when he finally slowed down a little, Doctor Weiss leaned forward and said softly, in English, "Mr. Lindsay, I thank you with all my heart, but I must give myself up. I cannot let Sister Josefa die for me."

Uncle Dick went on driving. "It is useless to give yourself up," he said without turning his head. "We have reason to think that Sister Josefa will get whatever help is possible, and I am sure hers was a considered decision. Frau Oberin is right. You must think about your family. They are waiting for you."

"Sister Josefa said a strange thing," Doctor Weiss murmured. " 'Your family needs you; mine will be better off without me.' I did not realize then what she intended."

"Right," Uncle Dick said curtly. "And now, Doctor Weiss, please sit on the floor, so you cannot be seen."

She obeyed immediately, sinking onto the floor, her hair barely touching the edge of the seat.

They were out of the old quarter of the city now, and

Uncle Dick stopped the car in a side street that looked almost deserted. "See that telephone booth on the corner?" he said to Ann. "Go and call this number." He read it off his cuff. "It's the inn at Sandplacken. I'm hoping that either Herr Weiss or Ilse will answer."

Ann looked doubtful. "Suppose the Gestapo man answers?"

"Then hang up. But otherwise say simply that we are coming to pick them up and that Doctor Weiss is safe and with us."

The telephone rang and rang. Ann had almost given up hope when someone at the other end finally lifted the receiver. There was a silence, and then Ilse's voice, trembling and almost inaudible, said, "Hello."

"Ilse," Ann whispered, "This is Ann. Is that man still with you?"

"No," the voice came back faintly, "we are all alone. The Gestapo man took the car of the inn, the one we were going to use and went off in it. We think he went to the village to eat. He kept opening cupboards and rummaging around, grumbling that there was no food. He left about five minutes ago and locked the door."

"Never mind, we will get you out. Now Ilse, listen." Ann glanced over her shoulder to make sure the door of the telephone booth was securely closed. "Your mother has not been arrested. She is here, with Uncle Dick and me. We are bringing her with us, and then we will all go on together."

She hung up without waiting for an answer, and hurried out.

"So far, so good," Uncle Dick said. "Let's hope that chap makes a hearty meal of it."

The car shot forward. Ann clasped her hands and

studied the tips of her fingers. Her heart lurched every time the car took a sharp turn.

"We should be close to Sandplacken now," Uncle Dick said at last. "Wake up, Ann. What's the matter with you? Do you recognize this place? Where do I turn off?"

Ann looked out of the window. The big boulder by the roadside seemed familiar. "The dirt road begins over there," she said, pointing at the group of pines.

When the roof of the inn appeared above the trees, Uncle Dick stopped the car. "Stay inside, please," he told Doctor Weiss. "And keep hidden. I must find out if the coast is clear. Ann, you can come if you want, but you must keep out of sight of the inn."

"What are you going to do if the man has come back?" Ann asked, hurrying after him and slithering on the wet pine needles.

"Oh, I'll just say I'm an American tourist and did not realize the place was closed. Then we'll have to think of something to lure him away. Don't come any farther now. I'll go on alone."

It seemed an eternity to Ann, but could not have been more than a couple of minutes before he reappeared. "Here they come," he said.

Herr Weiss and the girls appeared round the bend of the path, walking hand in hand. Rachel had Morritz's lead. Ilse was leading her father because one of his eyes was completely closed by the swelling and the other was obviously damaged. As they came up to Ann and Uncle Dick, Herr Weiss said hoarsely, "She is . . . ?"

"Just down there, in the car," said Uncle Dick. "She is waiting for you."

Ann started to follow, but Uncle Dick put a restraining hand on her shoulder. "Give them a minute," he said. "This is the first time in months that they have been together, and it may well be the last."

Ann stiffened. "The last?"

Uncle Dick took his pipe out of his pocket and carefully packed and lit it. "It could be," he answered, throwing the match down and stamping it out. "No use closing our eyes to the fact that we have less than a fifty-fifty chance of making it to the border without being stopped. Let's get moving!"

Herr Weiss was standing by the car. "Herr Lindsay," he said, clearing his throat. "We owe to you our lives."

"Later, later," Uncle Dick interrupted him. "We're not there yet. We must get out of here before the Gestapo get back."

"I can't understand why he left us alone in the first place," Herr Weiss said nervously. "He must have realized that with the windows so low it would be easy to get out."

"But where could you have gone?" Uncle Dick reminded him. "Half blinded, with a small child and with little or no money. He was not running much of a risk. Now, everybody into the car, please. Herr Weiss, you sit in the back with the girls. Take the dog with you. Ann, you sit in front as before. Doctor Weiss, I am afraid you must remain sitting, or rather lying on the floor. We will have to cover you with a blanket, so that you won't be seen if we happen to meet a police car before we reach the Swiss border."

Doctor Weiss raised her strained white face. "Herr Lindsay, why should you and your niece risk your lives for us? We could try and get shelter somewhere in Frankfurt, if you will be so kind as to drive us there. But the Swiss border! You must realize how little chance there is of our reaching it."

"There's more of a chance than you might think," Uncle Dick answered. "The most important factor is how long it is going to take the Gestapo to find out they have the wrong woman in their hands. Ann tells me that Sister Josefa is not unlike you in looks, so it may take them some time—enough to give us a few hours' start. The second factor is that the Gestapo knows about the air reservations Herr Weiss has made so they will be looking for you at the airport. In any case, whatever is for or against us, Ann and I are certainly not going to back out now!"

Producing a blanket from the trunk of the car, Uncle Dick spread it over Doctor Weiss. "Pull it over your knees," he told Herr Weiss. "Good. In this weather it looks quite natural."

Everything was ready. Uncle Dick and Herr Weiss consulted briefly about the route. "We could save about fifty miles by going back in the direction of Frankfurt but bypassing it and driving through Bad Homburg," Herr Weiss suggested, but Uncle Dick would not hear of it. "Much too risky," he said. "Let's go through Konigstein. It's a roundabout way, but it's the one the Gestapo is least likely to suspect." He glanced at the road map spread on the seat between him and Ann. "So, we'll take the road to Oberreinfenberg. We're off!"

As the car sped along the narrow road through the pinewoods, Ann thrust her hands deep into the sleeves of her coat. The rain had stopped, but it was getting colder and the sky was rapidly turning a threatening white color. It could mean snow.

194

20

The Swiss Border

The sandy, rain-soaked road was bad. The wheels of the car constantly bounced over potholes and at each jerk Uncle Dick winced slightly, although he was obviously doing his best not to let Ann notice. Herr Weiss assured him that the road would be better after the Rotekreuz crossroads.

In the back seat, Herr Weiss and Ilse were talking to Doctor Weiss in whispers. She was telling them how Frau Oberin had felt sure no one would find her, dressed in a nun's habit. Even when the Gestapo came, Frau Oberin had remained composed and when they asked to see the nuns' identification cards, she produced the cards belonging to two nuns who were in the city hospital, so that both Doctor Weiss and Sister Josefa were accounted for.

But then one of the Gestapo men had found Doctor Weiss's diploma. She could not bear to destroy it, so it was hidden inside a large missal. It proved to be a fatal mistake.

The mention of Doctor Weiss's diploma reminded Ann of Doctor Fromm. "I'm sorry we weren't able to call the doctor and let him know about our leaving," she said, but Uncle Dick only frowned. "The good doctor would never have let me leave the hospital, and *drive,* into the bargain. Besides, it is better for him and for Frau Meixner not to be mixed up in our departure. No doubt they are anxious, but it can't be helped."

The crossroads sign appeared and the road became smoother. The white sky was very low now. Wind beat against the car windows in such fierce gusts that Ann was afraid the windows would cave in. Then sleet came, clogging the windshield so that Ann had to get out of the car twice to clean the glass with her muffler because the windshield wiper could not cope with it.

When Konigstein came in sight, Uncle Dick slowed the car down and turned to Herr Weiss. "You say you know this town quite well. Can you route us through back streets where we're less likely to be seen?"

Herr Weiss peered through the window, squinting his good eye. "Turn left here," he said. "It will take us round the outskirts, rather than through the center. But why should anyone connect your car with my wife?"

"The Gestapo could," Uncle Dick answered grimly. "They know I am connected, through Ann. I keep hoping that the hospital will be the last place they will think about, as I never really was in the picture. However, if they do decide to check on me, it will take them only a few minutes to find that I am gone and then trace the license number through the garage."

No one said a word, but an extra chill seemed to pass through the car.

Uncle Dick increased speed. Konigstein came and went. It was almost dark outside. Cars whizzed past, their headlights picking up the long streaks of sleet, and disappeared in the distance.

Without looking up from the road, Uncle Dick asked Ann, "Do you think that small car is following us, or is it my imagination?"

Ann was just beginning to relax a little. In the darkness one could not see the road flying away under the car's wheels and the queer feeling in the pit of her stomach was beginning to pass. At her uncle's words, she sat up, rigid, and turned to look through the rear window.

"Southward now, in the direction of Mainz," Herr Weiss directed.

Uncle Dick muttered, "If we can make it. There *is* a car following us. Right, Ann?"

She only nodded.

Nearer, nearer . . . "It's catching up with us," Ann murmured. "Uncle Dick, what are we going to do?"

"Face whoever it is and see what happens. We have no choice."

Pulling in to the side of the road, Uncle Dick slowed the car almost to a crawl. The car behind was gaining rapidly, its headlights blindingly close. "It is stopping," came Ilse's agonized whisper.

Brakes screeched. There was the sound of a window being rolled down, and an elderly man's voice asked, "Could you please tell me how to get to Mainz? I am a stranger in these parts and the weather . . ."

The wind carried the last words away. Ann sat back

and let out a long breath. Herr Weiss, obviously trying to keep his voice steady, gave directions. The man said, *"Danke schon,"* and his car vanished into the night.

Suddenly, Ilse began to giggle. "I was so sure it was the Gestapo chasing us," she gasped between the giggles. "And it was only an old man . . . an old man." She kept giggling and repeating, "An old man."

A hand reached from under the blanket and Doctor Weiss said, "That is enough, darling." Ilse gasped once more and became silent. Rachel was already asleep.

Herr Weiss asked, "How is the road?"

Uncle Dick's answer was not reassuring. "Slush now, but it is going to turn icy before long. It is getting colder."

The car was rapidly coasting downhill. They were leaving the Taunus mountains. Ann looked at her watch. Almost six. Uncle Dick was right. Tiny snowflakes were already dancing in the beams of light. Ann watched them until she became drowsy. She vaguely heard Herr Weiss say something about Mainz and was dimly aware that they were driving over a bridge. Wasn't it the place where the Main and the Rhine merged? She tried to remember, but could not. Yet she could visualize the page in her geography book describing the area. She could even see the blot of ink in the middle of the page. Strange that the blot was getting bigger . . . and bigger. . . .

She woke up because the swift steady movement of the car was no longer there. They had halted by the roadside. Uncle Dick was sitting in a strange way, hunched over the wheel. He was breathing in gasps, and by the light reflecting from the road she could see that his face was covered with sweat.

"Uncle Dick! What's the matter?"

He tried to smile. "It looks as though the good doctor was right," he said. He paused a moment without speaking before continuing, "I'm afraid Herr Weiss will have to take over the wheel. It's just not possible for me to go on driving."

"I would gladly drive," Herr Weiss said from the back, "but one eye I cannot use at all and the other is not so good. Would it not be better if my wife . . . ?"

"We daren't risk it. And Ann can't drive. So you are the only one. I will step out so that we can change places."

Uncle Dick opened the door and a gust of wind almost wrenched it from his hand. Very slowly he swung his legs out, and managed, by supporting himself against the car, to move toward the back seat. Ilse and Rachel were asleep, but Doctor Weiss helped to settle Uncle Dick in beside them.

"We are quite comfortable on the floor, Morritz and I," she said in reply to his apologies. "You should not have left the hospital, I know!"

"The wind is getting worse," Herr Weiss commented, climbing in beside Ann.

"Just as well," said Uncle Dick. "It sweeps the snow away instead of letting it accumulate. Otherwise it would be quite deep by now."

Ann was looking through the windshield. Nothing but darkness, the whirling flakes of snow, and, beyond the headlights, darkness again. How was Herr Weiss going to drive through this?

Much the same thoughts must have been passing through Herr Weiss's mind for he said helplessly, "I can barely distinguish the road."

"That is good enough," Uncle Dick spoke calmly.

"You drive and Ann will be your eyes."

"I?" Ann shot a frightened look over her shoulder. "But I can't see anything either. It's too dark."

"You will see better once the overhead light is out. Watch for the road signs, don't let Herr Weiss drive into the snow drifts, warn him if you see an ice patch ahead. We can't afford even a slight accident. I will supply the general directions." Somehow he had managed to unfold a road map on his lap and he now snapped on a small pocket flashlight. "We have just left Carlsruhe," he announced, consulting the map. "There's still a long way to go. Let's start."

The overhead light went out. The car moved, hiccupping, and zigzagging all over the road. Ann watched Herr Weiss's shaking hands tighten on the wheel as he tried to steady the car. After a desperate struggle he succeeded. The car still moved jerkily but at least it kept to a straight course. Something big lumbered past them. Ann was not sure whether it was a truck or a bus. Everything beyond the reach of the headlights was just a shadow. It gave her the eerie feeling of driving into nowhere.

On they went. Uncle Dick named the towns they passed, or mostly skirted for safety's sake, but the names meant nothing to Ann—they were ghost towns, hidden behind the curtain of snow. Her eyes were accustomed to the darkness now, and she thought she could distinguish the black outline of towering mountains. Schwarzwald? She did not really care. The important thing was to keep her eyes on the road and maintain the steady flow of instructions to Herr Weiss. "Keep to the right, that car is trying to pass us . . . Careful, there is a big branch lying in the road . . . We are coming to a turn . . ." Every nerve in her body was quivering, but she knew that if she

200

tried to relax even for a minute, she would break down and burst into tears.

Lights shone in the distance. "Freiburg," Uncle Dick said.

Herr Weiss murmured wearily, "So it is." The car ploughed on through the snow, still bearing southward.

Bad Krozingen . . . Mullheim . . . "We are getting closer," Uncle Dick remarked. "About time, too. It's almost three in the morning."

We've been on the road for almost twelve hours, Ann thought. Not that it made any difference. She still became numb with fear every time a passing car slowed down.

When they had gone through the town of Schliengen, Uncle Dick said, "We will reach the Swiss border in a very short time now. Shall we wake everybody up?"

Doctor Weiss's voice, rather muffled, said, "I am not asleep," and Ilse echoed, "I'm not either, but I don't want to move because Rachel is asleep with her head on my shoulder."

"Let her sleep," said her mother softly.

"Do you have the passports, Herr Weiss?" said Uncle Dick.

"Our three," Herr Weiss assured him. "Thank goodness Ilse had them, or the Gestapo would have taken them away when they took my wallet."

"I have my passport, too," said Doctor Weiss, "though we will not use it on this side. It has my Swiss visa in it."

"Good," said Uncle Dick. "You will need it when we are on the other side of the border."

"Look!" exclaimed Ilse.

Ann saw a bright light shining through the snow. Some distance away, another light, a dusky red one, was flashing on and off. The Swiss border.

Out of the corner of her eye, she saw Uncle Dick trying to sit up. Doctor Weiss reached out a helping hand but he said quickly, "Please, Doctor Weiss. Lie down flat. Don't move or make a sound. Try not to breathe if you can. I really mean it. Herr Weiss, have the passports ready, but let me do the talking as much as possible." He seemed to hesitate before he added, "There is a chance, of course, that the Gestapo has already called this particular border patrol and ordered them to hold us when we arrive. We will find out in a minute. *Go on.*"

A small wooden house with a corrugated iron roof came in sight suddenly, as if it had emerged from under the ground. Ladderlike metal steps covered with snow led to a narrow door. The only window was lighted. Another and much stronger beam came from a powerful searchlight on top of a post.

The car was still a few feet away from the house when a man in a gray uniform came out, holding his hand up. Herr Weiss stopped with a jerk that almost threw Ilse off her seat and woke up Rachel. Ann heard Uncle Dick's involuntary gasp of pain.

The man came down the steps and approached the car. Uncle Dick rolled down the window on his side and a very red face appeared in it. There was a strong smell of liquor. The members of the German border patrol were apparently warming themselves up.

"Passports, *bitte,*" the man said in a thick voice.

Uncle Dick gave him his own and Ann's documents. "Mm . . ." the small eyes under the blonde lashes skimmed each passport without interest. "British . . . *In Ordnung.*"

He thrust the passports back into Uncle Dick's hand

and bent down to get a better look through the window. "There are more here," he said suspiciously. "How many? Three? Is that all? Better turn on the light."

"Burned out," Uncle Dick lied glibly. "Here are their passports." Reaching out, he took the passports from Herr Weiss and presented them to the man.

"Ha! Juden," the man spat out. The amiable expression vanished from his face, to be replaced by a sneer. The sleepy eyes became alert. He examined each passport over and over again. His lower lip stuck out, he seemed to ponder over every word. Still holding the passports, he slipped his free hand into his trouser pocket.

Half-turned in her seat, her hands clutching her sleet-sodden muffler, Ann watched his every movement. He was pulling something out . . . It was . . . cold perspiration broke out at the nape of her neck . . . it was a big electric flashlight.

A strong beam of light picked out Herr Weiss's thin face and Ilse's terror-filled eyes, swept across Rachel and stopped at Morritz, who growled warningly. Ilse's trembling fingers closed around the dog's muzzle, stifling the growl.

The patrolman scowled. "You must have a health certificate for the animal to get him over the border," he warned.

"That is for the Swiss officials to worry about," Uncle Dick snapped, but Herr Weiss put in quickly, "We have it."

"So, so . . ." the man mumbled. He stood leaning against the car, the passports in one hand, the flashlight in the other.

Rachel began to whimper. Uncle Dick said impatiently, "Look here, you are freezing the child and the rest of us too, with that open window. You can see that the passports are all in order. May we go, please?"

"*Ein Moment, bitte.*" The patrolman began to thumb through the passports again. Ann counted the seconds . . . one, two, three, four. . . . Was he never going to finish? If only there had been a line of cars behind them, all impatiently honking for their turn! But behind there was only the deserted road. And somewhere, inside the patrol house, a telephone began to ring.

At last, the man finished with the passports. "All right. You may go. We don't want any Jews here." He almost threw the whole sheaf into Herr Weiss's face, then stepped back.

"Go!" Uncle Dick ordered tersely.

The car had barely moved, when the door of the patrol house flew open and a uniformed figure ran down the steps, shouting something. Ann could not catch the words, but they seemed to galvanize the man who had checked the passports. He flung himself in front of the car. "*Halt!*" he ordered.

Herr Weiss braked and Ann saw his hands tremble on the wheel.

"*No!*" It took Ann a few seconds to grasp that it was Herr Weiss speaking. Surprised, she looked at him. His hands were on the wheel again, holding it in a deadly grip. Stepping on the accelerator he drove the car straight at the man standing in the road.

The red face, distorted by shock and anger, flashed in front of the windshield. The man swore and jumped aside, but not before the right bumper picked him up and threw him several feet away on the roadside.

At the same time a shot rang out, followed by a tinkle of broken glass and a frightened child's scream. Ann shrank back as the windshield suddenly burst into a fine web of cracks. The car seemed to fly, its tires scarcely touching the ground, toward the black and white striped gate with the red light flashing above it. Dim figures dashed up from somewhere. The gate rose in the air and the car shot over the Swiss border. Herr Weiss shut off the motor, but they went on rolling for several feet before the car stopped.

Uncle Dick switched on the overhead light. The car was already surrounded by Swiss patrolmen, all talking at the same time, shouting and asking questions.

Uncle Dick ignored them. White as a sheet, his face contorted with pain, he still managed to lean toward Ann. "Are you all right?" he asked. "Sure? That bullet missed you by an inch." Ann looked with stupefaction at the round hole in the windshield.

Behind them Ilse was screaming, "Rachel is hurt! Look, she is bleeding!"

Doctor Weiss called desperately, "Help me out! Please!"

And then, rising above all the voices, came Rachel's frightened wail, "Mutti! Mutti! It hurts!"

Rachel? But she can't speak, Ann thought vaguely, watching Herr Weiss wrench the car door open and rush to his family.

Everybody was out at last and standing in the road. Doctor Weiss had Rachel in her arms. The child's hair was smeared with blood. She was sobbing and at the same time babbling something. Herr Weiss held Morritz's lead with one hand, while with the other he kept patting Ilse's shoulder, telling her over and over again, "Rachel is all right, my darling. She is not really hurt. It was just a graze."

"Looks as though it's back to hospital for me," said Uncle Dick wryly. He leaned heavily against the car. "But we did it!" He mustered quite a reasonable grin. "Look at that, now, Niece, Ward, and Sole Living Relative. We're not reporting history this time—we've made it!"

In front of them, the Weiss family were moving off toward the Swiss patrol house—united, and free.

21
Afterward

"We are only going to stay in Basel for a few days," Uncle Dick had said, but they stayed almost a month. Uncle Dick had to go back into hospital, and the Weisses decided not to go to England after all, but to wait for visas to the United States. "The farther away, the better," Herr Weiss said. "And our applications have been in so long that we ought to hear soon."

Rachel's wound healed almost immediately, and she talked all the time. The shock and sudden pain had caused the "spontaneous healing" that Doctor Fromm had hoped for. Ilse, too, looked healthier and calmer, and was obviously looking forward to their new life.

Almost at the end of their stay, Ann received a letter from Doctor Fromm. It had no return address on the envelope, and had been posted in Switzerland.

Liebchen, the doctor wrote, and then to Ann's relief, continued in English. *One of my old patients is going to Basel on business. I know I can trust him to post this letter. It is safer this way as it is very likely that my correspondence is being intercepted. I think you will want to know what happened on the day you left us and afterward. We speak often of you and of that time of stress.*

The doctor then described how he and Frau Meixner had almost gone out of their minds with anxiety when Ann had failed to return to Mylius Strasse. Later, when he heard that Uncle Dick had left the hospital, they became even more alarmed. At last, the doctor had decided to go to the convent to see Frau Oberin. He did not dare to use the telephone. He was not admitted, but Frau Oberin had come to the door and told him about the Gestapo raid. She ended with, "The English girl and her uncle have taken Doctor Weiss away. Only God can help them now." Frau Oberin had been arrested that very night, and next morning Frau Meixner and Doctor Fromm received summonses to appear at Gestapo headquarters for questioning.

But Colonel Von Waldenfels had interfered. He must have used a great deal of influence because Frau Oberin was released two days later, while Frau Meixner and the doctor were only asked a few questions and were not bothered again.

Strange are the ways of God, the doctor wrote. *The colonel saved strangers, but he could not save his own wife. She was sent to a concentration camp. The Gestapo assured him she would be released soon and allowed to leave Germany. But she has never come back. The colonel went to the camp himself to claim her, but was told she had been sent to another camp near Berlin. He tried again. She was not there and no one seemed to know what had become of her. Eleonore has been sent away to Bavaria, to her paternal grandmother, "for a change of air."*

All the news about the Von Waldenfels family, the doctor explained, was from Trudi. Frau Meixner contrived somehow to invite her for coffee and got the information out of her. She knew Ann would be interested.

As for Frau Meixner herself, the doctor wrote, she was seriously considering selling the house and moving to Canada where she had relatives. Peter was well again and back at school, but he was not happy there. *He spends most of his free time playing with the puppy Frau Meixner has got for him. It is a cheerful woolly mongrel and Peter adores him, but he still remembers Morritz.*

As to myself, the doctor went on, *I am going to retire soon and grow vegetables in some village in the Taunus mountains. I do not feel at home any more in Nazi Germany, but for someone who looks into the past, it is too late to seek another home abroad.*

The letter ended with good wishes to Uncle Dick and the Weiss family. There was just enough space left for the signature. The doctor had used every inch of the thin blue paper.

A few days later the Weisses finally received their American visas. Ann and Uncle Dick went to the station to see them off.

"Herr Lindsay," said Herr Weiss, shaking Uncle Dick warmly by the hand, "we know we can never repay the debt we owe to you and Anna. But when the war comes— as it surely will—would you consider sending Anna to us in America?"

Uncle Dick raised his eyebrows. Then he put his arm

around Ann. "Thank you," he said, smiling. "I would find it hard to give her up. But when war comes—and I agree that it is inevitable—who knows what will happen? Let us hope, at any rate, to meet again one day in a better, saner, freer world."

The whistle blew. The last kisses and good-byes were said. The train chugged slowly out of sight in the snow-clad landscape.

"Well, Niece, Ward, and Sole Living Relative," said Uncle Dick, *"now* what about heading for home?"

Temple Israel

Minneapolis, Minnesota

In Honor of the Bat Mitzvah of
SHERI OSTROV
By Her Parents
Dr. & Mrs. Charles Ostrov

October 20, 1979